SCARECROW

SPARROW MAN SERIES
BOOK THREE

M. R. PRITCHARD

SCARECROW is a work of fiction. Names, characters, places, and incidents either are the product of the author's imagination or are used fictitiously. Any resemblance to actual persons, living or dead, events, or locales is entirely coincidental.

Copyright © 2017, 2023 M. R. Pritchard

All rights reserved. No part of this book may be reproduced or transmitted in any form or by any means whatsoever without express written permission from the author, except in the case of brief quotations embodied in critical articles and reviews. Please refer all pertinent questions to the publisher. All rights reserved. No part of this book may be reproduced or transmitted in any form or by any means, electronic or mechanical, including photocopying, recording, or by an information storage and retrieval system—except by a reviewer who may quote brief passages in a review to be printed in a magazine or newspaper— without permission in writing from the publisher.

Second Edition 2023
Paperback ISBN: 978-1-957709-32-1

*Guard yourself
against evil temptations.*
—Fortune Cookie

Paradise by the Dashboard Light

There is a royal blue feather on my balcony; it's been there for days, stuck in the same place through rain, wind, and sun. It hasn't faded, it hasn't fluttered, it hasn't moved one goddamned millimeter. It's waiting for me to pick it up. A message, a warning, a love letter from a life I'm trying to run from. Been there for thirteen days. I'm not going to touch that fucking thing with a ten-foot pole.

I drink the last of my coffee, set the chipped mug in the sink, then grab my wallet and phone. I glance at the forbidden feather before closing the door to my hotel room.

It's late morning and already sweltering outside, not as hot as Heaven but close. Good thing is, it's not like back in Gouverneur. No one here cares what I wear. Everyone else is wearing bikinis and board shorts. I look perfectly normal.

I make my way across the elevated walkway of the motel, down the stairs, and head for my lawyer's office. Reuben Strong is the first lawyer I ever had that wasn't a public defender. A middle-aged dude with almost a sadder story than mine. He moved down to the islands after some big law firm in New York

City bent him over a barrel to show him the fifty states and forgot the lube. Seems New York City is pretty much the same on the earthen plane as it is in Hell. Who knew?

Reuben set up his agency in an old tourist shop. It looks out of place but has a great view of the ocean. I make it there in six minutes and let myself in. He's sitting behind a giant oak desk —reading my file, no doubt. He glances up at me over dark framed glasses. "You got yourself in some deep shit, Meg," is his greeting.

"You're telling me." I pace the spacious office.

"What kind of kid does this crap? You were arrested twenty times in one year for shoplifting."

I shrug. "I was bored." This big city lawyer has got to have seen worse than me. I attempt to change the subject, "What kind of a name is Reuben anyways?"

He groans. "I've told you at least fifty times, it's a family name."

"Never knew anyone called Reuben when I lived upstate. That's a sandwich, not a name."

"Should've checked downstate." He flips through my file. "You should have *been* downstate at a one of those centers where they scare kids straight. Jesus, your juvy record is thirty-seven pages long."

I stop, stand still. 37. There was a time when that meant something to me. Wasn't so long ago…

Route 37.

Old barn.

Snowy owl.

Reuben's eyes flick to me twice. "What's wrong?"

I shake it off. "Nothing."

"Is there anything you didn't do?"

"Thought that was sealed."

"Usually it is, until you do some bullshit like drive through border patrol in a stolen car, higher than a kite with blood on your shoes. What a shit storm."

"Well, I'm paying you a lot of money to clean that mess up."

Reuben leans back in his chair, runs his hands through his hair, focuses on me.

"What?"

"You're going to need a new wardrobe for court."

"What's wrong with my clothes?"

"You're wearing a tube top and those shorts are damn close to underwear."

"It's really hot outside."

"And all your..." he waves his hand instead of using words, "...is visible."

"They're called tattoos, prude."

Reuben shakes his head and mutters, "Girls like you have a name, and it's jailbait."

"Says the walking sandwich."

"It's a family name."

I sit across from him and look out the window. What kind of lawyer gets a beachfront office? It's absurd. The view is amazing; green-blue ocean, white sand, tall palm trees.

"You need something nicer. From a real department store."

"Fine." I cross my arms and glance at Reuben out of the corner of my eye. He's studying my file.

The guy is nice enough, took my case before I even asked him. All I did was walk in the door. He took one look at my picture on the television, one look at me, and said, "*Hell yes.*"

"Just one question," Reuben leans back and props his feet

up on his desk. "How'd you get from Canada to Key West so fast?"

"Magic."

His lips press in a straight line.

"You wouldn't believe me if I told you the truth."

He drops his feet to the floor. "You walked in my door five days after crashing through customs. The entire country was looking for you."

"Must've been a miracle." I raise my palms to the sky; control the urge to mention God. I don't tell Reuben the part where I stopped in the Bahamas before coming to Key West to find a lawyer. That would just involve another round of questions. I don't feel like explaining my life story to this guy. I don't feel like explaining it to myself half the time.

"The judge is going to want to know."

"Can I plead the fifth?" Explaining my ability to *poof* between realms might make his head explode.

"No."

"I'll have to make up some story then."

"Meg, you can't lie to a judge." Reuben is leaning forward now, focused on me, trying to hold in a scolding or something.

I shrug.

"You can't." He throws his hands down on the desk. "You can't just make some shit up. You will be under oath, your hand on the damn Bible. You have to tell the truth."

"The truth." I laugh.

"Yes."

"*You can't handle the truth.*" I include air quotes then glance out the window again, eager to get out of this office now that it's become the *seventh circle of questioning hell*.

"Try me."

"My name is Meg Clark." I stand. "I killed my mother the day I was born. My father is the Archangel Gabriel. My grandfather is Lucifer. I've done some very bad things. I even own a blade that was forged in the fires of Hell."

"Have you been watching Lord of the Rings?" He doesn't sound impressed at all.

"You wanted the truth."

Reuben's face is slack. I think he's trying to figure out if he'd rather laugh or throw me out of his office. "That's some dark shit."

"Yeah. And it's not even the half of it." I don't even go into the story of Nightingale and how I fucked her life up, or Noah.

Damn, I miss them.

I walk toward the window and stand in the full sun that's shining through. The darkness is strong today and it's gonna take a whole hell of a lot of liquor to quell.

"I should probably go." I head for the door.

"Come back in a few days." Reuben waves. "And stay out of trouble."

I SIT on the beach until happy hour, trying to ignore the sounds of the tropical parrots and seabirds. I try to remember that I'm in paradise; there will be no bitter winters here, no kerosene fumes, no hostile angels, no terrifying Hellions, no parental units interfering in my life. No... Sparrow. My eyes start to burn which is a clear indication that I must start with my nightly inebriation.

I stand, walk away from the ocean and head for the sidewalk. I control the urge to take off my flip-flops and soak in the heat of the concrete that's been collecting the sun's warmth all day. I almost miss the sweltering heat of Heaven, would nearly put up with it if that meant I could have Nightingale or Noah back in my life.

The walk to the bar that I frequent is short. I pass beach houses painted obnoxious colors, cheap hotels, and shops selling plastic crap from China. I flick the ring on my left hand with my thumb; the one Sparrow gave me for Christmas. It's started turning my finger green. I can't wear it every day like I used to.

I open the door to Sal's Bar, make my way to the far end of the counter, order the same thing as every night: four shots of Fireball.

I pace myself; take a shot every six minutes. By the fifth one the numbing heat reaches my cheekbones. The burn will take over my brain in no time. I order four more. The bartender only brings me two.

"More," I say, trying hard not to slur my words.

"Signs are clear. When you start breathing fire, I stop serving. Want water?"

I don't want water! I want to clean myself from the inside out, burn the stench of Hell off me with liquor fumes; the stench I can't seem to get clean of, no matter how many times I shower. No matter how many different bars of soap I use, the scent of woodsmoke and pine is embedded in my skin. It's discouraging, knowing that you smell like Hell and you can't rub it out.

"Give me a goddamn drink."

"Gave you six already." He tosses the bar rag over his shoulder. "Signs are clear."

"Fuck the signs."

Heaven starts playing on the jukebox. Bryan Adam's voice is smooth as the devil. *Son of a bitch*. Some teeny-boppers on the other side of the bar squeal with excitement, like this song has some meaning to them besides an idea of what it was like growing up back then.

"See?" The bartender pours a tumbler of water and sets it in front of me. "That's a sign. You'll be in Heaven in no time, damaging your liver like you do each night."

"You really know how to suck the fun out of life." I drop a fifty on the bar top and walk out.

The humidity of night is stifling. If it weren't for the ocean breeze, I'd think I was in Heaven with Remiel trying to push me under his thumb. The Fireball doesn't quell that memory, it's too easy remembering turning feral, sucking the life out of my boyfriend's father, Nightingale watching the entire time.

On my way back to my motel room, I stop at the liquor store and get a six-pack of beer. On an impulse I buy four packs of Hostess cupcakes too. Then I head for home.

Home. Used to be a place I was searching endlessly for, now I'm running from it.

I pass a group of teenagers on my way up the stairs to the second level of the motel. Reminds me of days with Noah, sneaking out to do sinful acts. I dig in my pocket for my key and open the door.

This place is nothing special. Not like that Hilton in New York. It does look like someone tried, there's a dark oak headboard and matching desk, but the makeover stopped at the living area furniture which is still white wicker.

I drop the beer and cupcakes on the coffee table, kick off my flip-flops, and settle on the couch to watch the sunset from the front room windows. I turn the TV on for background noise; makes me feel like I'm not so alone.

It takes the full six-pack to bring on that numb feeling that I enjoy so much. My mind stops racing. The thoughts of Sparrow and Noah and Nightingale end. I don't even think of Gabriel or Teari, or my mother and Lucifer. There are no feathers on my mind, no walking sacks of flesh, no bastard Council members. It's freeing, and incredibly lonely.

Maybe tomorrow I'll put all my money to good use and buy some friends. Can't be too hard in a place like this. Everyone wants to party and I'd like the blood flowing through my veins to be 160 proof. Yeah, I'll do that.

The dreams keep me up at night. Every time I drift off, Nightingale shows up. She's always whispering shit in my ear. I've got staying awake down to a science now though. I force myself to wake up just before she tries to take over my head. Works well enough. But I'm always tired the next day, exhausted really.

I stand, stumble to the bedroom, trip and fall across the bed.

This is good. This is very good. Nightingale has yet to be able to break into my drunken brain. Avoiding her is going to cost me plenty of liver cells.

I wake just after midnight, my stomach sour and head throbbing. I use the flashlight on my nightstand to illuminate the balcony. The royal blue feather is still there; been fourteen days now. While the palm trees bend and shake under the force of the night wind, that feather sits still as a stone.

I click the flashlight off.

Can't sleep.

I turn on the TV. *Shawshank Redemption* is playing, again.

It's become my favorite movie, remembering bits and pieces of this flick from my childhood was what helped me get out of that prison of the dead. Andy Dufresne taught me all I needed to know about escaping a locked cell. If there's any God I should worship, I've come to the conclusion that it is him.

But the scene of that damn dead pigeon brings tears to my eyes, always does. I get up and crack another beer, drink myself numb, drink until the thought of a bird no longer stabs my soul.

Goddamned birds.

I KILL time shopping until it's time to head to Sal's again. I buy nice jeans, sparkly tops and a pantsuit for court; clothes that might make me friend material. The shoe aisle brings me trouble. There's a pair of sparkling white Keds that are screaming my name. I buy two pairs and a pair of black heels for court. I'm not a banker but I'm positive that I've spent more money these past weeks than I've ever worked for.

After I've spent too much of my inheritance on cheap clothing, I head back to the motel and change clothes before heading to Sal's.

Buying friends isn't as easy as I thought it would be. Sure they all hoot and holler when they hear their drinks are paid for, but not one of those assholes makes it a point to come over and say thanks.

The beat of the jukebox begins to drown out the noise of the crowd. I glance at my reflection in the mirror behind the bar. I don't look much different than I did a few years ago. Still get carded when I buy beer.

I come to the conclusion that I am incredibly bored. Maybe I should get a job?

My cell phone jingles.

There's a text from Reuben.

I give up on trying to buy friends and go see him.

"We're going to practice courtroom banter," he warns when I walk in his office.

"If we must." I cross the room.

"You smell like a bar." He wrinkles his nose.

"I happen to like the smell of bars."

"Just make sure you don't smell like in in court."

"Scout's honor." I'm hoping they can't smell the dregs of Hell clinging to my skin.

Reuben sighs. "Let's get started. Do you solemnly swear that you will tell the truth, the whole truth, and nothing but the truth, so help you God?" He's holding out a thick book with gold edged pages and black leather binding. "Put your right hand on the bible."

He might as well ask me to stick my hand up an elephant's butt. "No."

"The judge is going to make you do it. If you try now, it will make it easier."

"I'm not going to swear on the bible. It's bullshit."

He looks annoyed. "Meg."

"Reuben." I cross my arms. "Not touching it. Don't need to. If you repeat a lie often enough, it becomes the truth." Sounds good to me.

"No one likes a smart ass. Let's do this. Now." This is the most serious I've ever seen Reuben.

I can't put my hand on that bible. Said it before, I can't believe in a God that would allow the things that happened during my childhood. Doesn't matter if I was a product of the ethereal realms, I was on *His* dirt, *He* allowed all that crap to go on as far as I'm concerned. I take it all very personally.

"Not happening, Reub." I walk out the door and head home.

———

I LAY in bed all day and stare at the feather on my balcony until the sun goes down. Before heading to Sal's, I shower and pull on a pair of dark jeans, a white tank top and a pair of my new Keds.

I have one goal for tonight: get numb and dumb.

The walk is quiet.

The streets are bare.

Sal's is empty.

I sit in a booth at the back, and place my order with a waitress. I get three shots of Fireball down my throat when Reuben walks in the door. He makes his way toward me and he doesn't look happy.

"Why are you here?" I ask, expecting a verbal lashing after refusing to lay my filthy hands on the bible and walking out on him.

"News."

"Great."

"What's wrong with you?" he asks.

"Got a bad case of liberosis."

Reuben stares at me, expecting an explanation, I guess.

"I've let the strong desire to care less about trivial crap take over." I down a shot. "It's freeing. You should try it." That's a lie. There's nothing trivial in my life, only a lot of heavy shit.

Still, it sounds like a good excuse, and I find the best lies are told with a smile and sarcasm. He doesn't need to know the darkness I harbor.

Reuben sits across from me.

"What are you doing?" I ask.

"Celebrating." The tone of his voice is borderline pissed.

"Thought we had court in the morning."

He laughs. It's hollow, apprehensive. "Would have had court in the morning. But a miracle happened about an hour ago." Reuben waves down the waitress and orders himself a shot of rum.

I lean back and wait for an explanation.

He claps. "Congratulations, Meg. The judge threw your case out."

I blink. "No shit."

"Yup." The waitress sets his shot glass down. "Strangest goddamned thing I've ever been part of. Called me on the phone, said the evidence was circumstantial and he didn't have time for it in his court. I could even hear the shredder going in the background." Reuben downs the shot, sucks in air between his teeth. "I think he shredded everything."

"Wow."

"Course, not sure how video from border patrol is circumstantial." Reuben throws back his rum, downs it in one swallow. "I was really going to *make it* with your case. Show those fuckers in New York what they lost."

I tap my fingers on the table. The lacquer's turned tacky with the evening humidity. "You worried about getting paid?" I ask. "I'll still pay you."

His eyebrows rise in interest.

"Really," I promise. It wouldn't be the first time I've tried to buy a friend.

"Thanks, Meg. And congrats. You're a free bird."

I choke a little on my drink.

Long moments pass, in which we simply drink and avoid eye contact.

"We should celebrate," Reuben finally says as he rubs his face.

His cheeks are already red. I doubt his kind of celebration and my kind of celebration require a lot less hard liquor.

"Sure." I've got nothing better to do besides find new ways to keep myself awake. "What do you have in mind?"

"There's a place a few blocks from here."

"Should I go home and change first?" I ask.

Reuben looks me over. "Nah. For the first time ever you might actually be overdressed." He stands, offers his hand. "Come on."

I stand and walk around his hand. "Don't take it personal. I don't touch anyone."

Reuben shoves his hand in his pocket. "Suit yourself. My hand is super soft."

"Never seen a day of hard labor?" I mock.

"Meh." He shrugs and laughs.

WE WALK SIDE BY SIDE, Reuben with his hands in his pockets, me with my arms swinging and keeping the perfect amount of distance between us.

I watch Reuben out of the corner of my eye. I haven't seen him out from behind that desk much. He's a good enough looking guy, totally metro though. He's fit, like he works out a few times a week or eats endless salads. I bet myself ten dollars that he'll be boning a beach bunny who's on vacation tonight. Probably a married one. He's a lawyer and I still haven't decided if he's got a soul. As far as I'm concerned, no lawyer from New York City has one.

"Where are we going?" I ask.

"Sloppy Joe's." He glances at me. "If that's okay with you."

"As long as they have a liquor license, I don't care."

The bar is brick, the name lit up in red neon. The place is packed with revelers standing on the sidewalk. Girls in barely-there skirts and off the shoulder tops and dudes sweating it out in jeans.

I follow Reuben as he makes his way in and over to the bar. As he's flagging down the bartender, my eyes are drawn to the center of the dance floor. There's a wicked tall guy there, his body moving to the throbbing beat of the music. He's all shadows and muscle, dark hair that nearly reaches his shoulders. The girls have flocked to him, their hands are touching the bare skin of his muscular arms. They rub their asses against his narrow hips. If I didn't know better, I'd say the guy was soaked in catnip, or vodka. Maybe he's a stripper and we're crashing a party?

"Meg," Reuben touches my shoulder. "What do you want, a margarita or something?"

"No, I want—" The guy at the center of the dance floor suddenly turns. His eyes are green, Ireland grass green. I recognize him in an instant. It's Sparrow.

I control the urge to cut every single hand off the strumpets currently mauling him. I left my blade at home, but I consider breaking a glass and using a shard in its place.

The sea of women parts as he walks toward me. Hands grasp at him, they bow, fall to their knees, worship him like he's a God or something. The bastard is doing this on purpose; punishing me for running and avoiding him all these weeks. He's trying to make me jealous. It's working. Sparrow is mine and I am his and... this is fucked up beyond repair.

Sparrow moves closer, he invades my personal space. I back up until I hit the bar.

Reuben steps closer. "Meg, is everything—"

"Go away, Scarecrow," Sparrow growls.

Reuben is gone, drowned in the crowd without another word.

Sparrow's hands land on the bar, trapping me between his arms. His head dips, lips brush my ear. "It's hard to be invincible together when we're not *together*."

I shiver. "It's hard to be together when you're sitting to the right hand of Lucifer."

He smiles. It's dark, promising, and hotter than any smile I've ever seen on another dude. "He's your grandfather."

"Thanks for reminding me."

"I've missed you, Meg. Took too long to find you."

Sparrow is looking totally hot, even without the batwings and Hellion getup that's not visible on the Earthen plane. I must work hard to remind myself that he's part demon now, Hellion actually, everything I don't like about Hell.

I can't play this game. I must make it clear we've reached the point of no return and remind him of all the reasons he has to hate me. "I killed your father, ruined your sister."

The bartender drops a glass. During the time that it takes for the shards of glass come to their final resting place, Sparrow has his hands on my waist and he's dragging me to the middle of the dance floor.

I guess shock and awe didn't work.

The band is playing Bon Jovi's *Runaway*. Sparrow's humming, swaying; his hands move to my hips, guiding me right along to the beat with him. I haven't danced with Sparrow since we were in Heaven and I was having my debut ball. That seems like so long ago. We danced nothing like this, bodies grinding close together. That was a proper snooty, hands-on-the-shoulders-and-the-hips kind of dance. I like this kind better.

Sparrow moves his leg between mine and starts dancing like we're in a dirty movie. This feels too good. Nobody has touched me in weeks. I give up, give in, let the darkness take over and touch him. The music changes to something newer, a pop tune with a deep beat. Sparrow never stops moving, never stops grinding against my lady parts. Sweat drips down my back. His hands are touching my body, places where there's ink hidden under my clothes. He's focused on the tattoo on my chest.

"It doesn't have to be like this," he whispers close to my ear.

"It can't be like it was."

I spent weeks locked in a bedroom, nothing but Sparrow's dinner. And he treated me like crap. I still haven't forgiven him for that. I still haven't forgiven him for forgetting who I was and what he promised me. I barely care if his scrambled brains were a result of him changing into a Hellion. It has been real sincere of him, trying to cure his family's curse and all.

He tips his head, birdlike and perfectly Sparrow.

"Why are you here?" I spin to dance with my backside rubbing against his groin.

Sparrow's large hands are on my shoulders; they slide down my arms, to my hips and press me against his crotch.

I tip my head. His lips are on my neck.

"I'm hungry, Meg." He licks the skin over my jugular. "Get us out of here. I can't control it for much longer."

"You can *poof* now." Ever since he drank my blood. After I drained and killed his father by sucking every last drop of blood out of his body, Sparrow can travel between realms just like me.

"I'll take you somewhere you don't want to go. Probably lock you up deep in a cave and keep you to myself. I'm giving you a choice. Get us out of here. Now."

Poof—we're in my hotel room.

Sparrow glances around. "Slumming it?"

The phrase sounds strange coming out of his mouth. Seems he's picked up on some slang since he's been in Hell.

"I'm embracing my trailer park roots once again. Can take the girl out of the trailer, but not the trailer out of the girl."

"You can do better than this." He moves to check the locks on the door and windows. "You deserve better than this."

"Whatever—"

Before I can utter another word, Sparrow is in front of me, unbuttoning my jeans, pushing them to the floor, ripping my sleeveless top to shreds.

"I paid good money for that."

"Doubt it."

He's right. I got it on clearance for four dollars.

"Ah, Meg, I've waited so long."

I point a finger to his chest, push him away, and hold him at arm's length. "First. Have you been feeding from Bloodwhores?" I can't stand the idea of Sparrow touching another woman. I don't care if he needs blood to survive now that he's a Hellion. I'm selfish like that.

"Never," he says.

"A promise is a promise." Sparrow's words that I can't help but repeat.

"I can't touch them. Never could. There's only you."

He must be drinking blood from storage, which means he's not as strong as he should be. He looks damn strong to me, felt that way when he tore my bra off a few moments ago.

Sparrow's hands keep removing my clothes. When I'm left standing in front of him in just my underwear, he stops.

"You're not armed." Sparrow glances around the room. "Where's the blade?"

"It's here. Hidden."

"You should have it close. Always."

"I can't walk around Key West with a blade strapped to my thigh. That might be cool in the otherworldly realms but not here. Just get me in more trouble. I probably need a permit or some crap to carry that around."

"You're not as far from Hell as you think. Not as far from Heaven either. Keep it close."

"Sure."

"Promise, Meg. A promise is a promise."

"Promise."

His lips are on mine, strong and firm, tongue spearing into my mouth to explore. That's all it takes for me to melt, to forget everything. That's what Sparrow does to me; he is my hallelujah, heroin, and reason to breathe. He is mine and I am his and no guy has ever felt like this in my arms.

Sparrow's hands are on my skin, his fingers applying pressure in just the right places. His mouth moves to my neck. I grip his shoulders, wishing that I could see the leather of his wings but they're not visible on this plane. I feel the sharp pinch of his teeth, his fingers moving inside me, the bulge of his erection pressing against my stomach.

As my fingers are working at getting his pants off, Sparrow's mouth is moving, licking and sucking my most sensitive places. Pressure is coiling in my stomach and I'm so close... I shove Sparrow away.

"Take your pants off," I instruct. "Everything off now."

His smile is dark as he does what I say. He strips the cloth away from his body and I am reminded of his Bon Jovi striptease in Heaven. There is something less innocent about this moment though. Since Sparrow went dark, I'd be surprised if there's one speck of purity left in him. The hollows and planes of his body are just like I remember.

"Don't make me wait," he warns. "It's been weeks." He runs his hands through his hair, groans like he's barely hanging on, standing across the room from me, both of us wearing nothing but skin. His muscles taut, eyes closed, back arched and... shit, he looks like a woman's wet dream. I blink, snap a mental image and put a pin in that shit for later.

I make him wait. I haven't forgotten him being a grade-A toolbag to me while we were in Hell. I want to make him suffer. Doesn't matter if his brains were scrambled and Jim blocked his memories with some dark magic. Sparrow was the one person I trusted, and he hurt me.

"You want this?" I run my finger down the outline of my jugular, across my chest, around the sparrow tattoo over my heart, between my breasts. I spin on my toes, give him a good look at my backside, bend over to tease—

I'm suddenly on the bed, hands and knees pressing into the mattress and Sparrow covering my back. I can feel the length of him on the back of my thigh.

"You shouldn't torment me. I can barely control myself." He sucks my earlobe into his hot mouth, pinches it between his teeth.

"Oh..." I arch my back.

Sparrow sinks his teeth into my shoulder as he thrusts.

Oh, this is sinful. The things he does to me, things he never did when he was pure Angel. Things I never did when I thought I was pure human. I give in, pressing my teeth to his shoulder and drink my fill. I haven't tasted blood on my tongue in weeks, nearly forgot the satisfaction.

Later, just as I'm drifting off to sleep, Sparrow's humming *Always*. There's my old Sparrow man.

SOMEONE IS POUNDING on the door to my hotel room. It's a thunderous hammering; the side of a fist, *bam bam bam*. Sounds like the cops. I sit up straight, roll out of bed, and stumble to the door. After unhooking the chain, I crack the door open and see a familiar face.

"What do you want, Reuben?"

"Came to make sure you were still alive. One minute we were ordering drinks the next, poof, you were gone."

If only he knew.

"I'm fine." I rub my face.

"What's wrong—" Reuben focuses on my neck. "Did that guy bite you?" He points to the bite marks.

I slap a hand over my neck. "No. No, of course not. I cut myself shaving."

"Your face?" He looks repulsed but I'm not explaining a thing.

"Whatever. I'm going back to sleep. See you later." I slam the door in his face and drag myself back to bed.

The bed isn't as soft as the beds I had on each end of the celestial spectrum, the sheets not as soft. I pull the comforter over my head and wish I had a manservant again to get me a bacon, egg and cheese on a biscuit and some coffee.

The toilet flushes.

I sit up straight.

Sparrow exits the bathroom. He's so tall that he has to stoop under the doorframe. Sweet Lord, he's not wearing a scrap of fabric. My heart pounds and I am instantly reminded of every sinful thing he did to me. Bloodfest '99 was all up in this bitch last night. I remember this shame as well; I want to melt into the bed. I've never been completely comfortable with my need for blood. I guess it's more of a desire since I can live without it.

"Good morning." Sparrow rounds the bed, settles down next to me. "That thing at the door—"

"My lawyer."

"Lawyer?" He looks confused.

"The law thinks I did some things," I say. "My mugshot was plastered all over the news for a while. It wasn't pretty."

I wait for Sparrow to ask what happened to me when I stepped through that forbidden portal to search for his sister. The things me and Noah did… If he knows, he says nothing.

Sparrow's tracing the stars tattooed on my shoulder. "You shouldn't trust him."

"We are on the Earthen plane, it's not all Angels and Demons trying to end my life."

"You're always running, Meg." He changes the subject.

"You've run from yourself before. It always catches up. I tried running from destiny, it turned out badly, both times."

I think that's the most lucid thing Sparrow has said since he became a Hellion. Heck, since I met him.

"I knew who I was," I say." I was comfortable being poor white trash. But this new person, what we truly are, it's hard to accept; hard to get completely comfortable in this skin." I shudder, trying not to think about it. "Did Lucifer tell you when you'll be done down there?" I ask.

Sparrow's hand stops moving. "I don't think it's that easy."

Well, that's disappointing. He's been acting as a Hellion for months now. I was hoping there was a designated amount of time for his term.

"I want you to be done with this," I say. "I want you to come back to me." I look away. I don't like people looking at me when I tell the truth, I feel too exposed.

"Come back with me," he says.

It's not that easy.

I put up with a lot of bullshit in my life but this thing between me and Sparrow is messed up. I'm still mad at him, mad at the world, mad at the ethereal realms.

I want him to leave.

I want him to stay.

"I think you've spent plenty of time down there," I say.

"We don't get to decide. Your grandfather does."

The fear I experienced when Lucifer wrapped his wings around me and informed me of how badly I'd fucked up returns. I'll never shake that. I'll never forget that I made the biggest mistake of my life. I should have used that one wish to free Sparrow. Instead, I used it on his sister and screwed her life up even more.

I watch Sparrow as he moves away from the bed and starts getting dressed. He wears the uniform of Hell, and when he's fully clothed and stands from lacing his boots, I want to rip it all off him and drag him to bed again. Him putting on all that leather is better than any other man dressing in a suit and tie.

"You're leaving?" I ask.

Maybe I made him mad. Maybe it's better this way, separate, worlds away from each other. In Heaven we were kept apart, in Hell I didn't know who he was, maybe the Earthen plane is where it all makes sense, maybe this is where we belong?

"Been gone too long already," Sparrow says. "Lucifer will have my hide when I return."

I bite the insides of my cheeks, try to hold in how pissed I am that Sparrow was recruited to be my grandfather's head demon. Bad things happened in Hell. All we were trying to do was free Sparrow's family of the curse, but shit got real fucked up. We killed a lot of Hellions, and then Sparrow killed Lucifer's scheming head demon, leaving Hell with a depleted policing force. And there is some ridiculous Treaty that says one realm cannot decimate another realm's policing force, so, here we are.

Sparrow rounds the bed and makes his way toward me. "You should sleep."

"I don't want to."

He kisses my forehead in a moment so sweet and innocent that it makes my soul ache.

Dream Weaver

My teeth hurt, specifically my lateral incisors. It feels like that one time John Lewis punched me in the face when I was sixteen after I mouthed back to him. I grit my teeth, feel pain, and then... that gritty sound like stone crumbling. My lateral incisor on the left breaks in half and falls out of my mouth into my open hand, bicuspids and molars follow until I've got a handful of broken teeth and I taste blood in my mouth.

Jesus Christ. I wake with a moan and sit up straight in bed and touch my teeth, wiggle them to make sure they're all intact. Goddamn Nightingale. And I was doing so good avoiding her from permeating my dreams.

I get up, shower, put on some clothes that smell clean, and then head to the local dentist, praying that they'll take a walk-in appointment.

After signing in and paying cash up front, I take a seat in the waiting room. I haven't been to the dentist in years, couldn't afford it as a kid, but I've worked hard to keep my teeth. Brushed every night, even flossed a few days a week.

"Meg," a short lady in pink scrubs calls.

I stand up and walk toward her.

"How are you doing today?" she asks.

"Great," I lie as I follow her to a small room.

"I see here that you haven't been to the dentist in a few years." She motions for me to sit in the dentist chair. "Are you having any problems with your teeth or did you just stop in for a cleaning?"

I lean back, lift my chin while she drapes a bib over me. "My teeth feel fine. I just keep having dreams that they're breaking and falling out of my mouth."

"Ah," she laughs, "we get that a lot here." The sound of her unpacking dental implements fills the room. "I looked up what it meant one time. One article on the internet said that it's a sign of costly compromise and lack of balance in your life."

"Sounds about right."

She rolls her chair to my side. "Open wide."

The next half an hour consists of her scraping my teeth clean and asking me questions that I can't answer, because she has her hands in my mouth.

"Did you want x-rays?" she asks when she's done. "It will give us an idea of what we can't see. Maybe it will put some of those dreams to rest."

I don't think x-rays will cure my problem, but it can't hurt. "Sure," I agree.

After, the hygienist shows me the x-rays on her computer screen when they're done. "Look," she points, "they're perfect. Nothing to worry about. Don't think your teeth will be falling out anytime within the next forty years or so."

"That's a relief." I might have to find Nightingale and choke her a little for that dream last night.

"You want to schedule your next appointment?" the hygienist asks.

I stand. "No. I'm just headed through the area. Won't be here long."

She walks me to the lobby and wishes me a good day. I run my tongue over my teeth and rejoice in how smooth they feel.

―――

On my walk back to the motel, I stop at a local sandwich shop and order a grilled cheese and orange soda. I eat it on the beach, intending to soak up the sun, but after I press my soda can into the sand to keep it upright, a rapid fluttering speeds around my head. I swat, thinking it's a flying beetle. It lands on my soda can and I get a good look at the thing. It's a hummingbird, tiny and iridescent green, with a fine long beak. It dips its beak into the opening of my soda. It seems to focus on me, blinking its beady black eyes.

"It's a creature that opens the heart. Brings love after pain." Teari is standing in front of me, my father's healer from Heaven, no doubt here to check up on me. She looks like an Angel even without her wings. She sits in the sand, cross-legged, wearing a pair of shorts and a bikini top that would put Nightingale to shame.

I bite my sandwich, chew and swallow.

The hummingbird stays perched on my soda can, taking frequent sips.

"What are you doing here?" I finally ask Teari.

"We've been looking for you."

"Who's we?"

"Your father and myself." She glances at the bird. "This little guy is a good sign."

I tip my head. "That bird is confused."

The hummingbird flicks its tiny tongue in protest.

"Why don't you come home, Meg?" Teari asks.

The hummingbird hops to my knee. I reach for the soda can and wash down the last of my grilled cheese.

"I don't have a home."

Teari tips her head to the side and blinks. "You'll always have a home in Heaven."

The bird feels like nothing on my knee. I have to stop myself from brushing it away and standing up.

"Nope. Not really ever." I glance around and notice that we're alone on the beach. "You should probably leave." This was my time for reflection with my clean teeth and memories of my night with Sparrow fresh in my mind.

"Have you seen Sparrow?" Teari asks.

"What's it to you?"

"Nightingale has news for him."

My spine stiffens. I bet it's bad news. Death in the family kind of news.

"No comment," I say. "But you should definitely leave."

"She's also upset that you keep blocking her." Teari scowls. "Or at least she was. I haven't been able to speak with her in a while."

"She's lucky I don't surprise her with a visit and pop her good in the throat."

"That would not be wise." Teari looks bored. She holds her finger out to the hummingbird. It glances at her before fluttering away. Teari frowns.

"Bet it's nothing personal." I stand, throw out my garbage in a nearby trash can, and begin to walk away.

When I turn around again, Teari is gone.

I WAKE to the sound of heavy mouth breathing and the stench of death. I shoot to my feet. There are three rotting sacks of flesh ambling about my hotel room and one is putzing around right in front of the closet door.

Good thing I moved my blade to the nightstand. I open the drawer and grab the blade gifted to me by Lucifer. The blade hums to life as the heads roll. I try to keep the wet thwacking sounds to a minimum and hope to hell that the room below me is empty.

At nine in the morning, I'm left with a bloody weapon and three headless bodies on the floor smelling like rotting meat.

Of all the bullshit—*Poof*—I flash to Hell.

Sparrow is standing in the middle of the Hellion lair.

"You can't just drop the walking dead on the earthen plane!" I yell at him. "They don't belong there. People are going to freak the fuck out. I'm freaking the fuck out."

"Come home," he replies; his tone is flat, uncaring. Pisses me off.

Even though the depths of Hell beckon me, I reply, "No."

Poof—I flash back to my motel room.

The bodies are still there, steaming and stinking.

Poof—Sparrow stumbles over one.

I spread my arms and motion to the sacks of flesh. "You can't just do this because you want me to go back."

Sparrow looks around. "I didn't send them."

"Then who did?" I hold back from screaming at him.

There's a knock on the door, a pounding, really.

"Great. That's probably the cops."

"Meg?" The voice outside the door is Reuben's.

"Go away, Scarecrow," Sparrow shouts as he starts collecting heads and arms.

"What the heck are you doing?" I ask.

"Taking them back. They can't be found here. If you disrupt the balance then God will cast you out of the earthen plane. This is His land. You'll have no choice, He will send you where you're wanted most. I want you with me, but there's a heck of a lot more people in Heaven who want your head on a stick. You can't just kill an Archangel on their ground and walk away."

Sparrow is standing in front of me, gripping three heads by their hair with one hand, and three bodies by their wrists with the other. Blood and ichor stain his skin.

"Meg!" Reuben shouts from outside my door.

What the heck is he doing here?

Sparrow makes a face of near pain. "I can't be around that thing." He tips his head to the door. "Come back to me." Sparrow kisses me quick on the lips before disappearing.

I shower and change my clothes. Surprisingly enough the dead didn't stain the carpet and the smell has nearly aired out.

Reuben is still pounding on my door.

I strap my blade to my thigh and open the door.

"What have you been doing?" Reuben looks worried.

"Starting my day with a bang." I slam the motel room door closed and start walking. I practically sprint my way to Sal's bar. Reuben follows me the entire way; strange thing is, he never says a word about what's going on in my motel room. I'm sure he could smell the stench and heard Sparrow's voice.

I slide onto a barstool. "Vodka. Tall one."

The bartender holds up a variety of glasses.

"The big one. The water glass," I tell him.

"Christ, Meg," Reuben sits next to me. "It's only eleven in the morning."

The bartender slides my order across the bar. I take a long drink of the vodka and try to wash the gagging scent of the dead out of my system. "It's Russia somewhere." I drain the glass, replay the events of the last few days, the words from Sparrow. Something is odd. My head snaps in Reuben's direction. "Got a question for you, Reub."

While I was drowning my worries in a liter of vodka, he managed to obtain a bottle of beer. "Shoot," he says between sips.

"Why does he call you Scarecrow?"

Reuben sets his glass down, turns his head, the motion and his wide grin reminding me of a horror flick. It's sinister. "Peel me to the bone and find out what you see."

I stand, tip the barstool over, and grasp my blade.

"There's a bounty on your head. Huge one." Reuben drains his beer before standing, taking his time. Everything about him is suddenly menacing; his flannel shirt, skinny jeans, and Chucks. To think, I felt sorry for the poor bastard. Seems I have a problem with picking friends.

I back away, glancing at the bartender who's cleaning glasses like nothing strange is going on.

"Who sent you?"

Reuben wipes his mouth. "The Deacons."

"Fuck."

"Yup." Reuben launches himself at me.

I run, step up on a booth bench and leap across the tabletops to get away from him.

Reuben laughs. "Nothing personal, Meg. They're just trying to buy their way back into Heaven." He grabs my ankle. "Rumor is you've got some explaining to do."

I fall, cracking my knee on the floor; pain springs up my arms as I catch myself from smacking my face. I kick at Reuben, get him good in the nose. I try to focus on where I want to go —*poof*—I'm back at my motel room. I scramble to pack my things. As I'm tossing my clothing and shoes in a suitcase, six walking fleshbags materialize out of the floor. I gag; their stench is unbearable. I slam my suitcase lid down and snap it shut. Every rotting neck turns and the moaning starts.

Crap. I glance around and make sure I've got everything. I flick my ring finger with my thumb. The ring Sparrow gave me is on the nightstand in the bedroom. I drag my suitcase with one hand, grip my blade with the other. Two of the walking sacks of flesh are between the ring and me. They groan, arms outstretched, mouths gaping and teeth snapping. I hated this part of Hell.

My blade hums to life and glows, it cuts through the bones of the dead like butter. I grab the ring and shove it in my pocket. There's one last thing: that royal blue feather is still waiting on the balcony. But I can't risk touching it now.

There's pounding on my door. "Oh, Meg!" It's Reuben's voice. "I'm not going to hurt you. Just need to take you on a little trip." He shoves at the door and breaks the lock but the chain holds the door. From the bedroom I see his eye peering through the crack in the door.

Shit. *Where do I go? Where do I go? Where do I go?*

I can't think. There's nothing fresh in my mind, and I've got to get miles away from Reuben, like the other side of the country away. There's only one place and I don't really want to go there, so I choose the next closest.

Poof.

I RETURN to the parlor where I got the sparrow tattoo. It was really the only place I could think of where I last felt comfortable in my own skin.

The tattoo guy is sitting behind the counter, seems shocked when I emerge but gets over it real fast. Me appearing out of thin air barely fazes the guy.

The lights flicker. During the milliseconds of darkness the tattoo guy looks like he's backlit with blue light. That happened last time I was here and I get the feeling it's not a coincidence.

"Oh hey, sparrow tattoo. How's the bird look?" he asks.

I pull my shirt down to reveal the watercolor ink of a sparrow in flight on my chest. "Perfect."

"Nice." He stands, rests his hands on the counter. "What can I do for you?" His face twists. "Name's Meg, right? Where's your friend?"

I release my suitcase and it falls to the floor with a thud. I cross the lobby, grab the tattoo guy by his shirt and pull him across the counter. "Who are you?" I ask. "Or *what* are you?"

He raises his hands, palms up. "Name's Jed." He sounds so innocent.

"Why do you glow blue?"

"You can see that?" He smirks. "Cool."

"Not cool. Spill it." I twist his shirt until it's tight around his neck.

"Okay. Okay. It's just that I'm in hiding."

"Why?" I twist tighter until the skin of his neck pinches.

"Whoa, whoa!" He twists his forearms revealing heavily tattooed skin. The ink looks familiar to me now; it looks just like the text that was chiseled into the arch of that forbidden Hellportal that Jim made.

"What are those?" I grab his arm and rotate it to inspect the ink.

"Runes. They're spells that hide me."

I release him, step back, grab my blade and hold him at arm's length, the point of my weapon pressing into the base of his neck.

"Explain. Now."

"Okay." He steps back. "Let me just close up shop so we don't get interrupted."

"Sure." I step away from the counter but keep my blade out and ready for action. This guy has a certain trustworthy vibe about him. But history proves that I can't trust my judgment.

Jed runs to the door, locks it, and flips the sign to *closed*. He pulls the shades on all the front windows.

"You're really tan," Jed says as he crosses the lobby. "I hope you put some SPF on that ink or it's going to fade. Of course, don't mind touching it up again."

"I was on vacation. I'll be pale as a ghost in no time."

"Did you happen to be in Key West?"

"Maybe."

"That explains it." The corner of his lip tips up as he walks behind the counter. He sets a small television set on the counter and turns the volume up.

CNN is playing video of a motel room, "*...the bodies of seven people were found in this motel room in Key West. Authorities say the bodies were decomposing and at least two were decapitated...*" Screams erupt in the background. The camera man pans the room, zooms in on one of the dead that I left behind. Its jaws are snapping as it crawls across the floor and sinks its teeth into one of the reporter's legs.

"And that, my friend, is the beginnings of Hell on earth. The blogs are erupting with murmurings of the zombie apocalypse." Jed flicks the television off. "That was you, right?"

"No. Kind of. Not really..." Oh, what's the use? "Yeah."

"What are you?" he asks.

"A mixed-blood mess." I secure my blade then sit down in one of the lobby chairs. I press my hands to my face and take a few deep breaths. "This is so fucked up."

I try to focus, figure out what to do next. Sparrow warned me that a higher power—who I don't believe in—will cast me out of the Earthen plane, but I can't go back to my father in Heaven, and my heart's too damaged to go back to Hell. Reuben is going to be looking for me with that bounty on my head. I bet he's already halfway here. I'm only a few hours from Gouverneur where I know there's a derelict Deacon, a Watcher from Hell, and a portal to the ethereal realms.

My head is spinning. "Do you have any hard liquor?"

"Bourbon," Jed offers.

I hate bourbon. "No thanks." My stomach rumbles.

"You probably shouldn't be drinking right now."

I rub my hands over my thighs. I think that maybe my ex Jim had a good idea when he dragged me all over the place during our engagement, buying that cabin in the woods and stocking up on supplies. I should buy a bunker; load up on guns and ammunition and booze.

"If you're running from Demons or Angels, I can help." Jed walks around the counter and moves closer to me. He points to the runes on his left arm. "This spell hides me from creatures of Hell." He points to a rune on his right arm. "This one hides me from Angels. They just see me as a normal human. One of God's creatures. Untouchable."

"Why are you hiding from them?"

"I am forbidden. My kind are slayed at birth." He tips his head. "Who are you hiding from?"

"Everyone. Everything. Heaven and Hell and myself."

"Well." Jed clucks his tongue. "That sucks."

It sure does.

"So, you want a new tattoo?" Jed asks. "I can't guarantee they'll work on you. I'm guessing you're a special case."

"Yeah. Yeah." I stand and take off my jacket. "Let's do it. But you should know that if you're screwing with me, I'll kill you in a heartbeat."

"Don't doubt that." Jed pats the parlor chair. "Everything about you screams badass crazy chick."

I'm not sure if that's a compliment or not, but I sit in the tattoo chair. Jed starts prepping my inner forearms. The earthen plane suddenly feels a lot less lonely, having someone who knows about Heaven and Hell.

"So what happened in Key West?" he asks.

"I got confused."

"That sometimes happens."

My stomach growls loudly.

"When's the last time you ate?" Jed asks as he works his needle.

"I've been consuming a steady diet of whiskey and vodka but I had a grilled cheese yesterday." I miss the beach; wonder if Teari is involved in this Scarecrow crap. "I'm always hungry." Plus, after fighting with Reuben and traveling, I'm going to be craving something with red blood cells.

Jed makes a noise. I glance down and notice his carotid thumping in his neck. My stomach growls louder.

"I guess we better get you some grub."

I lick my lips, remember the soothing taste of blood. Clea warned me the dark hunger will always be there, no matter how much I eat. I can never quell it, only distract it.

"Can we order, like, three pizzas?" I think for a moment. "Wait, is there still delivery up here?"

"Yeah. So far, the zombies are limited to Key West. And if you're paying, you can order as many pizzas as you want." He pats my arm with a towel. "I'm almost done with this one."

After finishing, Jed sets his tools down, takes off his gloves, and crosses the room to wash his hands. "What do you want, cheese?" he asks.

"Pepperoni on at least one." I dig in my pocket for my credit card. "Get some orange soda too."

Jed dials a pizza shop and orders. He tells them to use the back door when delivering. After setting the phone down, he turns to me, "They said almost an hour. We should just finish your other arm."

Jed gets started with the next rune. I try to focus on the sunburn-like sting of the new tattoo instead of the steady pulse of his arteries. Saliva fills my mouth. I stretch my neck to angle my face away from him. The minutes that pass are nearly painful. I've never been one for control but this, this I have to control. He's helping me. Still, there is the understanding that

I've felt this before. It's almost as bad as when Remiel had me locked up. Almost.

"This is done." Jed wipes my arm and turns it so I can see the rune clearly.

"Looks great." I jump out of the chair and cross the room.

He looks at me, surprised, maybe even a bit nervous.

I pace near the far wall. I try to control this insatiable hunger. I try to focus on the ache of the new tattoos instead of the dark craving threatening to overtake me.

There's a knock on the back door.

"That's lunch." Jed opens the door, gets the delivery and pays the tip in cash.

I eat an entire pizza myself and drink a full two-liter of orange soda.

"I guess you were hungry," Jed says as he chews.

"You have no idea." It wasn't blood, but like my mother said, food will do. It won't sate me but it will control the urge to do something else.

"How do your arms feel?" Jed motions to my new tattoos.

The black ink will be a stark contrast to my pale skin once this tan fades. "Fine. Barely feel a thing."

"Good." Jed takes a bite of his pizza, chews and swallows. "What happened to that tall dude in the Canadian tuxedo you were here with last time?"

"No longer on this plane." I stand.

"What plane is he on?"

I am silent.

Jed sets his pizza crust down in the box.

"I think it's best not to talk about it," I finally say.

"You owe me some information. I have the feeling that

getting mixed up with you is going to send me on the run again."

I take a deep breath. "Fine," I say. "My father is the Archangel Gabriel."

Jed nods in understanding.

"What about you?" I ask.

"Well, my father was an angel. My mother was human." His eyes narrow. "Your mother wasn't human, was she?"

"Not even close." I don't want to tell him that my mother is the daughter of Lucifer.

Jed starts eating again. "My birth was blasphemy."

"That makes two of us."

"I'm guessing that knowing you is going to create some trouble for me." Jed takes another slice. There's a knock on the front door of the shop, but after a few minutes the would-be customer gives up and walks away.

"I should probably get out of here."

"You want to use the back door?" Jed stands.

"Sure." I head to the lobby and get my suitcase. "Thanks for everything," I say as I'm headed toward the back door.

Jed smiles and tips his head. "Anything for a fellow forbidden creature."

Jed shoves the door open and we are greeted by a horde of the dead.

"Shit." Seems Jed doesn't have a rune to take care of these dead assholes.

"Close the door," I tell him. "I'll take care of them."

"Meg—"

"Do it!"

The door slams, the lock thumps into place.

I drop my suitcase.

Every head turns. There must be fifteen of them, crowding the alleyway, stinking up the place. The moaning starts, then the foot dragging. I reach for my blade and get to work.

Whoever is sending these is going easy on me. The dead are bags of bones, just flesh and grizzle, whatever meat they started with has melted away along with their clothing.

Heads roll, arms for the ones that get grabby. After a few minutes the pavement is littered with bodies, blood and ichor flowing toward the gutter. I holster my blade, run back to get my suitcase and then get the heck out of there.

―――

I RENT a hotel room at the Hilton nearby. Nothing fancy like before with Sparrow, just a double-bed and free breakfast in the morning.

I toss my suitcase on the bed and flip on the television.

"...authorities are on the lookout for what they suspect is a serial killer who is now dumping the decomposed bodies of their victims at various locations along the east coast..."

The screen zooms out to show the bodies littering the alley behind the tattoo shop; they show the hotel room in Key West again. The broadcaster looks young and full of life, so out of place standing next to the sacks of flesh sent from Hell to torment me. I shut off the television and head for the shower to wash off the fluids of the dead.

When I'm fresh and clean, I raid the mini bar. Get good and numb, stare out at the cloudy night sky for a long, long time and try to figure out where the heck I go from here. As I lie in bed, I bring my forearms together and match up the runes. I wonder if these will do any good?

My days are filled with travel. I use the main highways, stop at hotels with the vacancy signs off and beg them for a room, hoping that being in populated areas will keep the Scarecrow away.

I zig-zag across the state, take the bus to Rochester and rent a car. I take back roads to Syracuse and stay at a sketchy motel on the interstate, then it's across the state. I stop in Utica for lunch at an old-fashioned Italian restaurant that's so cozy I could live there. Then I move on to a bed and breakfast in Saratoga Springs. The place is a remodeled farmhouse on Crescent Ave, which sits on Lake Lonely—appropriate considering my current state; lonely and on the run, like the start to every bad horror movie ever made. Well. Not every one.

The bed and breakfast is clean and bright, surrounded by a white rail fence and English garden. I check in with a teenage girl at the desk. She's chewing on a piece of gum and flipping a magazine, looks like she'd rather be elsewhere. Me too, but this was the last place in town with a clean bed.

"Room one." She dangles a keycard in front of me, and points down the hall.

"Thanks." I grab the key and head to my room.

In the morning I'm going to switch out cars and then head to... hm, I'm not sure where to go. I could keep going north, head back to Canada or maybe drive to Alaska. That's if the Canadian government has forgiven me for blasting past the border. The judge threw my case out of court but I'm sure there are a lot of confused and pissed off people. People with a rap sheet as long as mine don't walk away from a case like that.

The rented room is all paisley print, white on white, and

glossy bead board paneling. I feel like I walked into a page of a Martha Stewart magazine. I toss my suitcase in a nearby chair and let that familiar feeling of not belonging take over.

From the open window, I hear a loon call from across the lake.

There's something I'm forgetting.

I know better than to return to the scene of the crime but I need answers.

Poof—I return to the motel in Key West.

The place is a ghost town. The sounds of gunshots fill the night. There's screaming, moaning, the whole town stinks of rotting meat. I think those bloggers are on to something, although I didn't expect to bring the zombie apocalypse down on the earthen plane. Whoever is doing this, I need them to stop.

The royal blue feather is still here. Still as a stone on the balcony. I step over stains on the carpet and grab a pair of tongs from the kitchenette. I return to the balcony and pick up the feather with the tongs. From what I remember of Sparrow's bird books, I think the feather is from a hyacinth macaw. It seems to be the right shade of tropical blue.

I hold my pocket open and use the tongs to tuck the feather inside. Who knows what the thing will do to me? Last time I touched an unsuspecting feather I woke up two days later. I can't risk that now, not while I'm on the run, not with Reuben looking for me.

Poof—I return to the bed and breakfast in Saratoga Springs.

The loon is still calling across the water; another's joined in.

I make my way to the sliding glass door on the opposite side of the room and open it. I step out onto the small porch, cross the decking, head across the backyard and down to the shoreline.

My boots sink into the soft, spring-moistened ground. I missed an entire season while I was in Hell and then in Florida. Not that anyone really cares about missing winter. Who misses twelve-foot snowbanks and black ice on the road? I shiver. I should have brought warmer clothes.

I barely care about the evening chill with the eerie tremolo of the loon beckoning me. A long, mournful wail echoes, followed by another as a pair of loons search for each other in the fog.

Maybe this place isn't so bad. Maybe I could just stay right here? I could drink my morning coffee on the shore and learn how to whistle the call of the loon like Sparrow and Nightingale can do so well.

There's a feather fluttering from between the rocks piled on the shore. I cross my arms to prevent myself from going after it. I can't trust a feather any longer; they only bring memories, heartache, and bullshit.

I stand by the water, listening to the call of my favorite bird until the sun goes down. The fog is thick now, creeping its way onto the lawn.

My cell phone rings. I pull it out of my pocket, don't recognize the number but I do recognize that it's a local Gouverneur number.

"Hello?" I answer.

"Hi... um, is this... Meg?" a woman's voice asks.

"Depends. Who's this?"

The woman on the other end exhales a breath. "She said you'd be wary." There's a pause, the sound of beeping in the background. "This is going to sound crazy, but a girl came to me in a dream, like, five times, and she just kept telling me to call you. She chanted your number over and over again. She told me that you needed to know what was happening. She said you could help."

Well, this is interesting. And she has no clue the crazy I've seen.

She clears her throat before talking again. "I just need you to come right away. She said you'd understand. She said you need to help guide him, that they couldn't help him anymore. The doctors can't fix him anymore." The woman sniffles.

"And who are we talking about?" I ask.

"Jack. Jack Cooper. I think you grew up with his little brother, Noah. At least that's what the girl said."

My heart thumps steadily in my chest. "What was this girl's name? The one who came to you in your dream?"

"It was... like, a bird's name, nut—no, mocking...—no, night... Oh, yes, that was it, Nightingale."

Something freezes up inside me. I haven't heard from Nightingale in a few days, not since I started running.

"What's your name?" I ask.

"Charlotte. Charlotte Cooper. Jack's, well, I'm his wife but we've been separated for months now." The beeping in the background gets faster, more frantic sounding. Footsteps thud on a hard floor. "Oh Jesus," her voice is muffled. "Can you come? I think you need to come now."

"Where?"

"Gouverneur County Hospital. I have to go. It's not good. Please, come quick."

She hangs up.

Well, that was interesting. I trudge back to my rented room, close the door to the porch, grab a jacket out of my suitcase, and—*poof*—I'm standing outside the County Hospital.

I head inside. I stop at the gift shop and order a coffee and purchase a blue stuffed teddy-bear with *Get Well Soon* stitched on its stomach. After checking in at the main desk and getting a name tag, I head to the ICU where they said Jack's room is. The lady at the desk said his room number with a frown, which makes me think that something really crappy is happening with him.

There's a woman in the hall. She's short, blonde, cute, just the type to marry a Cooper boy. She looks nervous as she spots me walking down the hall and waves.

"You're Meg." Charlotte says when I get close. "Now I remember you from high school."

I don't remember her. But I was doing my own thing in high school, I was too busy breaking the law with Noah and sleeping with my friend's boyfriends. You know, real ladylike stuff.

"Thanks for coming," Charlotte says. "I wasn't sure who else to call. He doesn't have any other family. Since Noah died it's only been us. But Jack, he just kind of, changed. Not long after the day you woke up. He didn't want to go to therapy, he didn't want to work on it. So, I left."

I've done some pretty shitty things in my life, but I don't think I'd ever do that to someone I—Oh, I did do that to Sparrow. He turned into a Neanderthal Hellion and I booked. Guess I'm not better.

"All they told me was that he was in an accident. No other details," Charlotte says. "I'm sure there's more to the story but no one will tell me anything."

Charlotte leads me to Jack's room. She opens the door and

motions for me to follow her in. There's a tube in his throat and two IVs in his hand. Even looking half-dead, he's still a handsome Cooper boy, light brown hair and dashing smile—if he could smile right now, if he weren't in a coma.

"Maybe you could spend some time with him. He was always telling me stories about you and Noah." She moves toward the door, clutching her purse to her stomach, a pack of cigarettes and a lighter gripped in one hand. "I'll be back later. I just—I just need some time." Her footsteps echo as she walks down the hall.

I sit in the cheap plastic hospital chair at the bedside and stare. Jack's hair is longer than when I last saw him, and his beard is growing in. The last I saw Jack he was stopping John Lewis from smothering me to death in my own hospital room. He also smacked John Lewis a little too hard with his billy club, sending the man who raised me to an early death and cursing himself. Jack took a life. If he dies, there's only one place he's going. I know Jack's going to Hell, unless he wakes up or he gets his ass to a Safe House and repents when his body finally gives up. I think it's best that he wakes up.

I break my usual rules and touch his hand. His thumb twitches.

What do you say to a man on life support? I don't know enough about Jack to tell him much.

When I was in a coma and my soul was trapped in Hell, I didn't know my solid body was still alive on the Earthen plane. That's what a near death experience will get you, a glimpse at where you're going. I wonder if anyone spoke to me when I was in a coma? I wonder if John Lewis whispered horrible things in my ear while I was knocked out with a tube down my throat? I had already killed my fiancée on the Earthen plane, there was no one that I loved to sit by my bedside and whisper words of encouragement to me. It's a miracle that I woke up at all.

"Jack?" I ask softly. Of course he doesn't answer, but there's movement under his eyelids. "Jack. If you can hear me," I lean closer and settle my elbows on the mattress next to him, "If you can hear me, Jack, wake up. Wake up. Wake up. Wake up."

Nothing happens. I squeeze his hand.

"Wake up, Jack!" I've been here five minutes and I'm already impatient. Maybe I should slap him? That always works in the movies.

"Is everything okay in here?" A nurse steps into the ICU room.

I glance at her. "It's fine."

"It's best you don't yell at that boy. His brain needs healing, quiet and rest and—" She rounds the bed. "You look familiar." Her lips press tight together as her eyes narrow on me.

"I get that a lot." I stand, getting ready to flee.

"I've seen you before. I never forget a patient. Oh, you're that girl who was in a coma here not so far back. Meg Clark, right?" She smiles wide. "It's a terrible thing that happened to you. But look at you now. What a miracle."

I tuck my hands in my pockets, pulling the left one out quick when I remember what's in there. "Yeah. That's me." I back away, toward the door. I don't need a happy reunion with all the nurses that wiped my ass. They're going to want hugs and shit and I'm not playing that game.

The nurse smiles and steps toward me. "It's so good to see you up and around and *alive*. We thought you were a goner. And the doc... after everything you went through. It's so nice to see you."

I take another step away. "It's fine. I'm fine. I actually have to go."

The nurse crosses her arms. "The rest of the team would love to see you. You should stay. I can call them down here."

"Maybe tomorrow." I bolt from the ICU room, walking as fast as I can without running off the unit, down the stairwell, and out the front door.

I turn the corner, head for a dark alley and—*poof*—I'm standing outside my hotel room in Saratoga again.

Just as I turn, stepping away from the darkness and fog of the lake, I come face to face with Reuben.

He punches me in the face. I drop. Mud seeps out of the ground under my weight, coating my knees and hands.

"How the fuck did you get here?"

"Jesus, Meg, you've used your credit card *everywhere*. The tattoo shop, the pizza place, the hotels, the car rental," he counts on his fingers. "I'd have to be blind not to follow that trail."

Well shit, it never occurred to me that maybe the Deacon's were technologically advanced. Is this how defeat feels? I should have known better. I watched Shawshank Redemption and all the Bourne movies a million times. I should've bought a fake ID or something.

"Doesn't matter how many runes you paint on your body. We know what your face looks like. Those marks will only hide you from those who haven't seen your mug shot." Reuben smiles. "Your face is hard to forget. Sometimes I dream about it, remembering your brown skin shining in the sun."

"I never liked you anyway," I say. "And I want a refund on the lawyer fees."

"I love the way you lie, Meg. You can't hide it, I know we

were besties for those few weeks." Reuben winks. "Life's a bitch." He glances down the alley. Fog surrounds us. He could slay me like a doe out here and no one would see it. "Time to travel. But first, I was ordered to injure you real good and make you weak so you can't flutter between realms at will."

I crawl away. "I won't. I promise." I've felt enough pain at the hands of others.

"This is definitely going to hurt you more than me." Reuben pulls a knife from his pocket. "I'd like to apologize, but you hit first. This is for that broken nose back as Sal's." He stabs me in the shoulder.

You never forget what it feels like to be stabbed. Barely feel a thing until the hilt of the blade hits home against your skin and you have time to process it all, the sharpness of metal on muscle, on bone. Similar to cutting raw chicken but a lot more blood. Also, it hurts like a bitch. I barely have a chance to moan in pain before Reuben grabs my wrist and starts dragging me across the yard then across the gravel parking lot to a car. He pops the trunk, bends to lift me up and deposits me inside.

"Sit tight," he smiles, "this ride's a short one."

He slams the trunk closed.

I roll to my back and press a hand over the wound on my shoulder to try and stop the bleeding.

The car starts moving. Reuben is a pretty shitty driver, he slams on the brakes, accelerates fast after stopping, takes turns going at least mach ten. By the time the car stops moving and I hear him turn the engine off, I think I'm bleeding more than when he first stabbed me.

The trunk opens. Reuben stands there smiling; he exhales a breath of exhilaration like he just did something really important.

"You're a shitty driver," I say.

"But did you die?" He smiles.

"I don't like you very much."

"It's freeing, finally able to be myself around you. No more lies." He reaches in, drags me up and into his arms. "No more dodging around what *you* really are." He turns.

We're in a graveyard. I've been here before. Crap.

"Always knew who you really were. It was great watching you try to hide it. You should never hide who you really are, Meg." He stops in front of a stone arch and drops my feet to the ground, keeping another arm across my shoulders. "Let's take you home."

Home. A curse word if I ever heard one.

Expect Angels, but Expect Nothing of Them

Reuben whispers ancient words and the space under the arch changes, like heat radiating off pavement in the summer; shimmery and opaque. He steps through the portal, dragging me along with him. We exit into a gleaming fertile desert city. There are two giant Angels guarding the portal on the other side, dressed in shining gold armor, blades longer than any I've seen before.

Two Deacons wait for us, also.

"Welcome to Babylon," Reuben says as he shoves my shoulder.

I stumble away from him, releasing the wound on my shoulder to catch my balance. Without the glamour of the earthen plane to hide what Reuben really is, I turn and get a good look at the real Reuben. There's a black void where his head should be, like one of those images of a black hole in space. His arms and legs are still moving, still interacting with the Deacons, and no one in the room seems to care that Reuben lacks a face but I can't hold back the gasp of shock.

"Scarecrows are creepy." I recognize Teari's voice.

I pull myself together and press my hand over the stab wound on my shoulder again, but blood has already dripped onto the gleaming white tile under my feet. "What are you doing here?" I ask.

"Keeping tabs." Teari grins. "Your hair's looking a little long." Her eyes zero in on my shoulder. "I'll fix that for you." Her hand touches my back; it's warm, reminds me of the sunny afternoons in Key West.

"Stop!"

Teari moves away, looking like she's been slapped.

"Do not heal her." A giant man with a bald head, white beard, and eyes darker than any shadow I've seen in Hell walks toward us.

"I apologize, Raguel." Teari bows her head. "I was merely—"

I've heard of this Archangel, he heads the Council and works with my father.

"You unholy thing." Raguel stares down at me. "Finally returned to pay for your sins."

"Not by choice." I tip my chin up.

He makes an expression of disgust, brow furrowed and cheek ticked. "Bring her to the prison," Raguel commands Teari.

She touches my shoulder again and leads me away from the elevated platform of the portal.

"Where is my father?" I ask when we get a few feet away.

"He can't help you here," Teari sounds concerned. "This is Babylon, the City of Heaven. It is surrounded by the Seven Kingdoms, neutral ground where the Council meets. Gabriel can speak his piece but I doubt he will be able to free you from this on his own."

"Wonderful."

Teari's hand is warm on my injured shoulder. "Keep walking. I'll heal you as we move."

"What are they going to do to me?"

"Lock you up. Bring you to trial for killing Remiel."

It's never worked. Sometimes you just must accept that you're bad to the bone.

"I don't understand why you can't just conform to one side or the other." Teari sounds disappointed. "It would've been easier if you were human and—"

My glare shuts her up. "If I never forget what I am, it can't be used to hurt me."

We arrive at a row of five clear boxes, one's empty. The other prisoners are winged men; their glorious wings look like they have mange, feathers litter the ground around them.

Thankfully I don't have wings.

"This is the prison?" I ask.

"Yes." Teari motions for me to step inside the empty box.

"Are we on exhibition or some crap?"

She nods. "Sins on display, so others will see and learn."

I step inside the box and feel frozen in place for an instant. A shackle snaps around my neck.

"It's enchanted," Teari warns. "So you can't flutter between realms." She holds her hand out. "Give me your blade."

"No." This is worse than any jail cell I ever stepped foot in as a kid. At least they took the shackles off there.

"Give it to me or someone else will take it. I'll keep the blade safe," she promises.

I give in, unstrap the blade from my thigh and pass it to her.

"Be good, Meg. There isn't any rock hammer or spoon

strong enough to get you out of this jail cell. Gabriel and I will work at getting you free."

I wonder if she was checking in on me and caught me watching all those *Shawshank* reruns?

The door slams closed and Teari walks away.

Not one surprised angelic face passes by my cell. I recognize some of the Angels from my father's realm as they walk by or stop to stare.

I sit on the floor cross-legged, rest my elbows on my knees, and try to figure out how the heck I'm going to get myself out of this mess. I've spent too much of my life behind bars. You'd think I'd learn a lesson. Or find a good hiding spot, at least.

The remainder of the day and a sleepless night follow with a lack of exciting events and mud and blood drying on my clothes. I check the stab wound from Reuben every few hours. The skin is bright pink and slightly puckered. Teari healed it the best she could.

By morning my cell is an oven with the heavenly sun beating down through the clear ceiling. I wipe sweat off my forehead and consider stripping down to my underwear to escape the heat.

Crowds of Angels walk by.

Gabriel finally shows. I stand and press my hands to the wall of my cell as he moves closer.

"Assholes." He slams a fist against the clear wall of my cell. "Have they fed you?"

"Not in days." I swallow, my throat dry and sore.

"Dicks. I'll have their balls in a vice for this stunt." He clenches his fist and holds it up high.

"It's fine," I say.

"Far from it." Gabriel's eyes are fiery blue. His fists are like giant hammers. Makes me wonder how I am half of this man yet so small in comparison.

Raguel is suddenly at my father's side.

"This is no way to treat kin of mine," Gabriel warns.

"Seems your kin is always causing trouble." Raguel tips his head in my direction. "But this abomination is the worst of them."

Gabriel's hand lands heavy on Raguel's shoulder, the two men turn away from me to converse.

I lean closer and hear Gabriel say, "We have to take her to Remiel's Kingdom. We have to try with *her*." It sounds like more of a command than a suggestion.

Raguel looks less than pleased when he turns to face me again. He points at my neck. "The shackle remains."

The door to my cell opens. I recognize Teari walking closer from across the sandy city center square.

"She had better return," Raguel warns. "She must pay for her sins."

Gabriel and Teari direct me toward a waiting Cadillac Escalade. I get in the back. There's a brown paper bag with a savory smell coming from it. My door closes and as Teari's getting in the passenger seat, she says, "That's for you, fresh from your father's kitchens."

Gabriel gets behind the wheel. The man looks much too large for this vehicle, looks like he's stuffed himself into a clown car.

Teari hands me a thermos.

As Gabriel starts driving, I open the bag and pull out French fries, a cheeseburger with bacon wrapped in wax paper, and a container with blueberry pie. I can't cram the food into my mouth fast enough.

Teari glances back at me. "When's the last time you ate?"

I push the food to my cheek. "Like, four days ago." The last I ate a real meal was when I was driving through Utica.

Teari makes a sound.

Gabriel glances at me in the rearview mirror.

I'm getting a vibe from them; I think they're worried. I am too after what I did to Remiel.

I eat every crumb in the lunch bag and drink whatever delicious beverage is in the thermos that tastes like grape soda.

Before I know it we're driving down an oak tree-lined road, Remiel's castle in front of us.

"I don't think this is a good idea," I mention to Gabriel and Teari. "The last time I was here things did not go well."

"It's the only thing we haven't tried." Gabriel turns off the vehicle.

Teari's door opens. "We think you can help." She opens my door and motions for me to get out.

They don't take me to the basement; thankfully, they walk me through the front door. There's dust on everything and the furniture is covered with sheets. We walk up a winding marble staircase and through a giant oak door in the hallway on the second level. We're in a bedroom. Nightingale is sleeping in the bed, her shoulders propped up on pillows, skin pale, and her roller skates at the foot of the bed resting on their sides.

"Try to wake her," Teari says.

I walk to the side of the bed. "Nightingale?" I call. "Nightingale... Night..." I shake her shoulder. "What's wrong with her?" Scanning her body, I notice a visible bulge in her stomach. I set my hand on it, feel the fluttering kick and know instantly. "Holy shit." I back away. "Hol—holy shit." Tears sting my eyes, guilt is a wave that threatens to drown me. My stomach threatens to heave up the meal I just ate. "Is that from the Hellions?"

Gabriel's arms are crossed, he looks deep in thought, doesn't answer my question.

"It could be," Teari finally answers. "Or it could be someone else's." She rounds the side of the bed opposite to me. "Who was she with in Hell?"

I shake my head, recall what went on. There was a lot of bird watching, Nightingale experiencing freedom out from under her father's thumb. "It was just us. She was rarely out of my sight or Noah's."

"Noah?" Gabriel moves toward me. "Your dead friend? Another one of those who marinated their souls with the sins of the earthen plane?"

I nod.

"Let's pray the child is his," Teari touches Nightingale's abdomen.

"Why won't she wake up?" I ask.

"Would you? If you were shithouse rat crazy and knew that you'd only pass it down to your child because of your family's curse, if everyone you loved were gone and you were left alone with a Kingdom to rule, would you wake up? She's pregnant with a child out of wedlock. That is forbidden in Heaven. For a woman it's worse, they will force her to marry as soon as she wakes. With her father dead and Sparrow serving his time in Hell, Nightingale is the Queen of Remiel's Kingdom," Gabriel answers. "It's a shit storm in the making."

"She refuses to leave the astral plane," Teari's hands hover over Nightingale's body, "only comes to us in dreams."

And I know why. "Noah's there."

Gabriel moves to the other side of the bed. "That explains it then."

"But he's a spirit, a spirit who belongs to Lucifer. How does this even happen?" I motion to her belly. "He's a ghost. Does he even have sperm?" I can't wrap my head around any of this. But it wouldn't be the first time that the happenings of the ethereal realms turned my world—and all reason—upside down.

"Better be careful, Meg. Things that aren't supposed to be happening have been happening." Teari looks worried.

The shackle around my neck constricts. I push my finger between the metal and my skin, trying to loosen it.

"Don't toy with that," Gabriel warns.

"It's tight."

Gabriel's lips press into a thin line. "We should return to Babylon." He motions to Teari. "Now that we know more."

The return to Babylon is sobering. Even with a full stomach, the knowledge of Nightingale's condition brings about memories I'd rather forget. Memories of Hellions knocking at my door, the death of my unborn daughter, the death of my fiancée.

"How long before the Council brings me to trial?" I ask as I watch Heaven pass by outside the window.

"I'll rush it along," Gabriel replies.

Teari turns in her seat. "Don't lose faith, Meg." She reaches back to touch me, but I move. Her hand hovers in the air for a moment before she turns away.

Gabriel glances at me again in the rearview mirror. He knows better, I never had an ounce of faith to lose in the first place.

Once we reach Babylon, my father returns me to my cell.

Teari stays in the vehicle. She's probably pissed because I

wouldn't let her touch me. The only reason I allowed it when I got here was because I knew she could heal me.

"What will they do with me?" I ask.

Gabriel frowns. "You will stand before the Council and answer for Remiel's death."

"I couldn't help it."

Gabriel frowns before he warns, "Some bad shit is going to happen. I can do nothing to stop it, for this I am sorry."

That sounds ominous. "What kinds of things?"

The door to my cell closes. Gabriel says nothing, unmistakable concern masking his face.

"What kind of things?" I ask again, pressing my hands against to wall of the cell. "Gabriel!"

Gabriel walks away without another word. I glance down the row of prisoners who are all watching me with vacant gazes.

THE NIGHT SPARES me from the intense heat of the day. I lie on my stone slab of a bed and stare up at the sky. Whimpers and moans come from the other prisoners. One of the Angels has lost all the feathers off his wings. He reminds me of when I found out what Sparrow actually was. I'll never forget him standing on that altar in Hell, revealing his broken and featherless scaffold of wing bones, proclaiming to me what he thought he was. The poor bastard was better off functioning as a cracked nut in Hell. And at most times, it seems I was better off in a coma, not knowing that my damaged soul was traversing Hellscape.

The door to my cell opens.

A large figure in a dark cloak stands outside. With the rise of his hand, the shackle around my neck tightens, lifts, and drags me out of bed and across the green lawn of Babylon. My toes scrape across the sidewalk as I am dragged to a large marble building and down a giant staircase that can only lead to one place. When things like this happen, the dark staircase never leads to a bright and airy room with a freshly cooked dinner. Never.

The smell of copper burns my nose, it makes the saliva swell in my mouth, reminds me that no matter how much food I eat, the hunger can only be sated by one thing. The tools hanging on the walls are intimidating, but not as much as the blood dripping from their action ends. I lick my lips and try not to stare as I am deposited in the center of the dungeon. Hm. I never expected a true dungeon in Heaven. What I knew of Angels growing up was that they were good, merciful even. Those childhood Angels never had a dungeon dripping in blood. It just shows how much we get wrong on the Earthen plane. If only those poor humans knew.

The hood comes off the dark figure standing in front of me. It's Raguel. I'm not the least bit surprised.

"Look what we have here," I mock. "Big bad Archangel dragging a *Mudblood* off to the dungeon. So typical. Saw this in about a hundred movies."

"You have guilt, fear, and worry about that foolish Nightingale and the dead from Hell turning the Earthen plane into a playground. I can sense it. You've spent too much time on that plane. You can't separate yourself from those humans. Your humanity is your handicap, girl."

I laugh. "I've been doing bad shit my whole life, don't think I have much humanity left."

I know it's a lie; when I was in Key West there was something that connected me to the beings of the Earthen plane. I can't deny it. I was birthed there and I spent my first twenty-five years amongst pure blood humans thinking I was just the same as them. I can't say that didn't affect me.

A whip slashes across my back. I hold in a scream. I want to laugh in Raguel's face. This is nothing compared to Jim stringing me up and stabbing me in the chest. Nothing compared to watching Sparrow suffer for me. Nothing physical could ever match that.

I wonder if this is some of the "bad shit" Gabriel warned me about?

Another lash comes down, stinging across my shoulder blades. Since I have no wings to take pride in, this must be Raguel's method of punishment. A crack erupts in the dungeon as another lash snaps across my lower back.

"Does it turn you on? Sick fuck, doing this to a mortal without wings. I bet you dreamed about it all those weeks I was in Hell. The best decision I ever made was to leave this shithole."

"You'd best learn how to shut your sinful mouth."

Another lash. Blood oozes down my back.

This is going to ruin my tattoos.

"Did no one tell you, Meg? You're as immortal as they come. I could whip your hide all night long and you'd live another day to tell the common folk of the earthen plane. Here in Babylon we believe in two things, discipline and the word of God."

Crack.

I bite my tongue.

"It would be easier if you had wings. Perhaps if you simply had one ounce of faith within that wicked hide, I wouldn't have to punish you like this. But, we all must pay for our sins."

Whipping a person has got to be the most sinful act, next to murder. Raguel's logic is all off.

This is not *Cell 14 of Cellblock 5*, this is not a dead-ridden cell in Hell, this is not juvy on the earthen plane, this is someplace much worse. Heaven is never described like this. What I wouldn't give to watch reruns in my motel room right now. Drinking myself into oblivion each night was better than this. At least I had control.

———

AFTER MY PUNISHMENT, I lay on the elevated stone slab in my cell, wishing Sparrow was here to lick my wounds closed. Blood pools under the small of my back. I can't control the low moan in my throat, but I don't cry. Girls like me don't cry, we get a beer and drown our worries. That's what I always say. I wish I had a beer; any hard liquor would do right about now.

The other prisoners are watching, probably waiting to hear me weep like I've heard them each night. I'll be damned if that happens. I need to figure a way out of this glass cell. *What would Andy Dufresne do?* I need that on a bracelet.

I hold up my forearms, the runes dark against my skin, and wonder how in the hell I'm going to get Jed to fix my back tattoos over scar tissue?

When I finally sleep, I dream of Nightingale. She's wearing a flowing gown that barely hides the bulge in her belly. She looks concerned.

"Come back," I beg her, hoping that she might be able to put in a good word for me. She was there when her father,

Remiel, locked me up. She could tell them what was really going on in that room in his basement.

Noah is there too, looking as handsome as ever. The endless galaxy is the background, no buildings, no land, no chairs for us to sit in and converse, just the three of us floating in space. The astral plane is vast.

"I can't leave him." Nightingale is crying. *"I can't do this alone."*

"You won't be alone," I argue.

"You know nothing of Heaven, the laws we live by, what I was trying to escape."

This is not the Nightingale I first met. The resilient girl who embraced her crazy has changed into a sobbing, red-eyed thing of worry.

"I'm there now, paying for all of our sins," I explain.

Nightingale looks shocked. She must not know that the Deacons captured me for a bounty.

I turn to face Noah. "Why couldn't you just leave her alone? Why did you have to do this to her?" I control the urge to fling myself at him and slap him around. Don't care if he's the best best friend I've ever had. I warned him to stay away from her when I brought her to Hell. I was just trying to help her escape her asshole of a father, I didn't mean for this all to happen.

All of this is too much.

I squeeze my eyes closed and rub them until I wake up, then I lay in the dark until the sun rises.

SPENDING the night with Raguel took its toll. By morning I'm hungry—starving. I can barely control it. The sun of Heaven was punishment enough, but now sweat is dripping into the lash wounds. It burns and stings, making it hard to focus.

The other prisoners watch me as I stalk the spectators. I am something feral, pacing my cell, blood dried to my torn clothing. I need to eat something. When the Angels get close I snap at them and show my fangs. I show them the monster that lurks in the shadows of my damned soul. Perhaps they were right to fear me. For the first time in my life, I'm so out of control that it scares me.

Before I have time to wallow in my own pity, the door of my cell opens. The invisible force of the shackle around my neck drags me out, down the path between cells, and through the center of Babylon at a snail's pace. My toes drag on the ground, the shackle tightens so that I can't speak a word. Something scrapes against my back and I feel the marks open and fresh blood ooze down my back.

Recalling what little I know of the bible, I find this ironic as... I can't even think of a good example right now. My head hurts, my back aches, and the void in the center of my soul is hungrier than it's ever been.

The Angels on the street stop what they're doing to watch.

I don't tip my head in shame, I tip my chin up, raise both hands and give all those fuckers the bird. My hands are forced to my sides after entering a marble building. I am set to my feet in a large courtroom.

A sharp gasp breaks the silence. Teari is sitting not far from me, her eyes locked on the marks on my back. It wasn't so long ago that she had reservations about healing me. She didn't give a crap who I was or what I'd been through, thought I was nothing more than a human in the wrong realm, thought I would do nothing more than bring Sparrow heartbreak. She was right about that, but he had his part in it all. He damn near broke my heart too.

There's a last supper-like table in front of me. Seven chairs but only six men. All the Archangels finally get to meet me face to face instead of simply bitching about me to my father.

Raguel is the first to open his ridiculous mouth. "Confess your sins to the courtroom."

My eyes flick to Gabriel.

"Not on your life," I say.

Raguel's giant, iridescent wings spread. "You will bow to the Lord Almighty. Pay your penance, accept His grace and be free. Now, confess."

"I am not a lamb in need of guidance. I confess nothing."

The other Archangels look bored. It seems my fate was sealed before I entered the room. So much for innocent until proven guilty in Heaven.

"So be it." Raguel continues. "You are banished from the Seven Kingdoms of Heaven. Banished to the cells of Babylon, not to be released until you have found—"

Gabriel finally stands. "You have no right!"

Raguel rises, gripping his blazing white blade. "You are outnumbered. Five to one. If Remiel's daughter were here she could voice her ballot, but since she's *indisposed* at the moment—"

"I'm going to dance on your ashes." Gabriel points his own blade at Raguel. "You will pay for this. She," his giant finger points in my direction, "is my child."

Raguel laughs. "This saga was created by your fevered loins. If you want to blame a soul, blame your own." He points at me as well. "*That* abomination should have never been born."

"You speak of loins," Gabriel's brows rise. "Let us measure

with all of Babylon to judge. My Kingdom is grander than any of yours." Gabriel grabs his crotch and drives his hips forward.

Teari's eyes are practically bugging out of her head.

I feel my own cheeks flame red.

The other Archangels sit up, taking in the spectacle.

"The greater Kingdom, the greater the vote." Gabriel looks like he's going to tear Raguel's face off. "Mine is bigger."

Raguel looks equally pissed, his face red and a vein bulging from the center of his bald head.

Someone clears their throat. The Archangels stop insulting each other for a moment.

"We have an idea." A Deacon steps forward. Reuben is right behind him, his black hole of a face watching me. "We can set this straight. We can take Meg back to Hell for a short time. With your blessing, of course."

"How would that cure anything?" Gabriel growls.

The Deacon smiles; it's sly, ugly. "There's been a death. An important death. The man who saved Meg's life on the earthen plane, Jack Cooper, has died."

Oh no, not Jack.

"Explain," Raguel looks generally interested.

"Jack Cooper committed the worst crime of all humankind, he murdered John Lewis, the man who raised Meg. It was unintentional, but still, murder is murder."

"Barely," I mutter. "And he was a demon, not a man. A good for nothing piece of trash."

Gabriel's eyes flash to mine, his expression is greater than any scolding I've ever had. My mouth snaps shut.

The Deacon continues, "Jack's soul is destined for Lucifer. But get him to repent, upset the balance. Due to the sin committed, his soul is one of the most valuable. We all win."

Gabriel crosses his arms. "The cost?"

The Deacon makes a motion, Brando from The Godfather years, "Four-hundred souls."

"That's preposterous!" Gabriel shouts.

The Deacon raises his palms innocently. "That's our offer. Take it or leave it. We have the Scarecrow to keep Meg focused. Without us you're at a loss. Lucifer wins everything."

The courtroom is silent. The six Archangels turn and murmur amongst themselves.

The waiting takes forever. Finally Raguel says, "The Scarecrow will accompany you and keep Sparrow away so he is not a distraction. Perhaps on this mission, he can help you find your faith. That's the only way we'll let you back in. An ethereal being without faith is nothing more than a human without a heartbeat."

Well, it's good to know that I am nothing more than a sack of flesh that's dead inside. I don't feel dead inside. I feel alive and fed up with Heaven.

We leave the courthouse and walk to the portal. The five Archangels in front of me, Gabriel and Teari flanking both sides of me and Reuben trailing behind with the Marlon Brando of all Deacons.

Teari leans close to me and whispers, "Find Jack. Seduce his soul to repent. Earn back your freedom." Her hand is on my back. "I can't heal all of this before you leave." With her free hand she passes me my blade.

I strap it on as we reach the portal. "Can I at least shower or change my clothes?"

Raguel shakes his head.

"Take this off." I point to the shackle around my neck.

"I can't do that," Raguel says. "We can't risk you disappearing on us."

"Let's go." Reuben takes my arm and tugs me in the direction of the portal.

WE STEP THROUGH THE PORTAL. My stomach roils as we travel through the planes, leaves on the wind only to be spit out into the bowels of Hell. Nausea is a bitch that leaves me stumbling, arms out to grasp something solid.

A hand grabs my upper arm. I rip myself away, stumble and turn. Holy hell. On this plane Reuben's dark hole of a face has been replaced with the smooth black head of a crow. I can't help but stare.

"Impressive, isn't it?" Reuben pets the side of his face, sleek with tiny feathers.

"What *are* you?" I can no longer control my facial expressions, which teeter between interest and disgust.

"I am the scarecrow." He stands proudly, fists on his hips like a superhero.

This is what I get for a sidekick. This is a mission I would prefer to complete with Sparrow at my side, not this Scarecrow, not this hay-man. And Raguel said I was empty inside; Reuben is so empty that he contorts depending on what plane he's on and what the Deacons want from him.

"Where do we find Jack?" Reuben asks.

We're standing in the middle of a crossroads. I glance around and try to figure out where we are. The street sign says Peabody Road, the cross sign labeled Little Bow Road.

"He'll probably run to his grandmother's house, just like I did."

"Why there?" Reuben asks.

"'Cause his brother stashed an assload of guns there."

That's the last place I want to go right now. Never return to the scene of the crime—that's where I met Sparrow. Going back there is going to be far worse than revisiting my house in Gouverneur and stepping over the bloodstained carpets and seeing that nursery that never held a baby. On second thought, maybe I'm wrong; maybe both experiences will be about the same.

"What does he need guns for?" Reuben asks.

Twigs snap from behind the nearby trees. It's daylight, which means the dead will be on the move.

I explain, "When you wake up here, the only logical thought is that you're in the middle of the zombie apocalypse. It takes a while to figure out that you're actually in Hell. So any human with a brain is going to search out weapons and shelter."

Jack's grandmother's house is on Birchwood. I start walking down Peabody Road, which eventually turns into Clinton Street. The snapping of twigs and rustling of leaves continues. The dead hear us and they're following. I walk faster, eager to outpace them.

"Where are you going so fast?" Reuben asks.

"I don't feel like getting mauled by the flesh bags. It's daylight, we need to get moving or find cover until nightfall."

I feel ashamed, walking down the street with a guy with a bird head. He looks as ridiculous as he sounds. I'd trade Reuben for a crazy Sparrow Man any day of my life again. Even if he's not the Sparrow I first met.

It's not long before we come across our first visitor. I

wondered how long it would take for someone else to realize we were here.

A few hundred yards down the road I see a floating pale figure. Dark hair, ruby red lips. Clea is here, my mother. The rustling from the forest stops as the dead keep their distance from her. The daughter of Lucifer, although dead, retains her power to keep the walking dead at bay.

"Child," she calls. "What are you doing here?"

I thrust a thumb in Reuben's direction. "On a mission."

"With that?" She eyes Reuben with interest.

"Unfortunately," I reply.

"And that?" Her eyes zero in on the shackle around my neck, she tips her head. "Why is that around your neck?"

"Angels." I try to push my finger between the metal and my skin but it's too tight.

Clea's eyes narrow. She circles me. "Is this their work as well?" She's looking at my back.

"Yup." My back still stings and oozes since Teari wasn't able to heal the wounds fully.

Clea places her hands over my chest and back, moves them downward until the ache from Raguel's whipping vanishes. The soreness of the wounds is replaced by an ebbing heat. I twist to get a glance at my tattoos. There's no scar tissue and it looks like I was never beaten by an Archangel on high.

"What did Gabriel say about this?" Clea asks as she circles to face me.

"He didn't know. But he wasn't happy when he found out."

"And that thing following you?" she whispers. "Who sent a Scarecrow?"

"The Deacons. So Sparrow can't get close," I warn. "So he won't *distract* me."

"He's been plenty distracted since you've been gone." Clea touches my arm. I step away. I can't handle being touched right know, not after Raguel. "Lucifer will be glad you're back. Sparrow will be able to focus on his work."

"What is his work?" I ask, but have a feeling I already know. When you sit to the right hand of Lucifer, there are only so many things that you can be responsible for, no doubt all of them dark and dangerous.

"I should tell them you're here," Clea changes the subject. "Maybe we can stop this." She disappears in a wisp.

I notice in the middle of the road is a neatly folded shirt and leather jacket. I remove the shreds of my blood-soaked shirt and pull the new one on.

Reuben looks around and peers into the nearby woods. "That's convenient," he says.

I can't get over the way Reuben's beak moves when he speaks.

"Better than walking around half-dressed." I pull the jacket on.

"For you."

Gross. I guess this is what you get when you buy your friends with money.

"Shut up." I walk faster.

"Who was that?" Reuben asks.

"My mother."

"Well, that explains a few things."

The dead are close enough that I can hear their open-mouthed breathing.

"Let's get moving." I start walking again.

Reuben follows behind.

The horde following us is thick, like someone knew we were coming and directed them all to Gouverneur.

We make it down Clinton Street then take a left at E. Barney, walking all the way to Rock Island. We outpace the dead, but not their moaning. I turn right, then take a left at Birchwood Drive.

Just like before, the big brick Victorian across from the school is calling me like a beacon, promising safety and comfort. Just like every grandma's house that ever was. The windows are still boarded up. We walk up the steps to the front porch. I reach for the door, hesitate for a moment, remembering what happened the last time I was here. The whole house turned, including Noah. The bodies are probably still inside, rotting, their jaws chomping at air hoping for a bite of meaty flesh.

A thud comes from behind the door.

"Can you check the window?" I ask Reuben.

"Nah. I'm good."

I turn to find him standing behind me with his hands in his pockets, staring off into space.

"What are you good for, Scarecrow?"

"Ca—caw!"

I jump. "What the fuck was that?"

"I'm good for scaring you." He smiles.

I've never seen a bird smile before, but he manages to change his expression, the tugging at his cheeks, the slightly open beak, it's the creepiest goddamn smile I've ever seen.

I turn away in disgust and shove the door open.

Whatever was thumping around in here has gone. Maybe it was a raccoon or something? The living room looks the same as the last time I was here. Floral patterned wallpaper, floral patterned couch and chair, mauve carpet. Jack and Noah's grandma had typical old lady decorating taste.

"Jack?" I call. "Jack, are you here?"

There's no response, only a hollow knocking and moaning coming from the basement. There were plenty of the dead left down there last time I was in this house. Knowing what's waiting in the basement, I head for the stairs to search the second floor.

The upstairs hallway is decorated in more old lady elegance. I search three bedrooms and two bathrooms and find nothing, not a soul lingers. I count my lucky stars that I don't find Jack already turned.

I bypass Reuben who's looking at a faded and cobwebbed black and white picture of Jack's grandmother and grandfather. I jog down the stairs, search the office, the half-bath and the kitchen. There's nothing. Just a quiet rustling from the cupboards that I already know will be vermin.

A thud echoes from the basement again.

My stomach growls.

"Come on, Meg." He leads me away from the door, down the hall, to the kitchen and through the door that I know leads to the basement.

I stop dead in my tracks. The last time I was led to a set of stairs, it turned out very badly for me. Noah must sense this because he stops and gives me a concerned look. I'm sure he heard what happened to me. News like that makes it across town before you're out of the operating room.

"I'm not going to hurt you, Meg. We just need to go somewhere safe."

I turn to look at him. This is my first interaction with real live people in weeks—no, months. "Noah?" I ask. His name sounds strange exiting my lips at this moment.

His brown eyes soften as he smiles. They're like chocolate, light milk chocolate. What I wouldn't give for a piece of chocolate right now.

"It's okay." Noah steps in front of me. "I'll go first."

He walks down the stairs, flicking the stairwell light on along the way. I hear people talking when he reaches the bottom.

GOD, I miss having Noah in my life.

Searching the basement is going to be a mistake. But I know there are rows of canned goods down there. Maybe even some leftover guns. If there's anything I remember about traversing the land of Hell, it's to be prepared. Since the Angels were generous enough to send me with nothing but my blade, I need supplies.

I take a chance and make my way down the dark staircase.

The dead are still down here as I expected, the girl who was giving Noah doe-eyes when I first showed up and the Asian kid, Rick. He's dragging himself across the floor. It's a sad sight, even if Rick was a dick to me when I first met him. I chop his head off and put him to rest. "Sorry Rick," I murmur.

Reuben follows. His movements are twitchy, like a seagull waiting for you to drop your lunch. He never lifts a finger to help.

I find an old backpack next to the couch. I empty out the musty clothes, keep the pocketknife that was tucked in the front pocket. I head for the shelving and select a few jars of canned goods, there's corn and tomatoes, pickles, and something that looks like it might be meat. I search for the last of Noah's guns. There were plenty that I left behind last time I was here. Under a shelf, I find a small handgun and a few bullets. My blade does a fine job at chopping heads but the gun could come in handy. I stuff it in the backpack.

I find a stash of weed and consider taking that as well. I take it. Maybe I can get birdbrain high and escape.

When I'm done the bag is heavy, but I'm a bit more prepared for a trek through the countryside of Hell.

"Jack's not here," Reuben says.

"Nope."

"Where's Jack's house?" Reuben asks.

"I'm not sure." I didn't keep track of the boys much after Jim came into my life and completely distracted me, didn't have much time to after my world went to shit. "But I know where to find it."

I head upstairs, search for the phone. Up in these north country parts the elderly never really caught on with cell phones, most of them still have and old-school handset with a cord next to the couch and—just as I expected—a Yellowpages phone book underneath. Back when I had my nice little house with a white-picket fence, the phone book went straight from the porch to the recycle bin, but not with these old people; they worship the phonebook like people my age worship Google.

I flip the thin pages of the phone book to *Cooper*, sliding my finger down the page until I find Jack and Charlotte. "There's an address on Battle Hill Road listed for Jack," I say. It's a place I remember as being a small farmhouse pushed back off the road.

If Jack stopped here first, the next person he'd go looking for would be his wife. I never really knew Charlotte, didn't even remember her from high school. I only know that every single lady in Gouverneur was probably crying in her pillow the night they wed. Noah was a good-looking guy, but Jack, Jack was a goldenboy complete with looks, charm, all of his natural teeth, and a real job. In a town like this, you don't find guys like that after the age of twenty-seven. I run my tongue over my own teeth, thankful that at the age of twenty-five, I've still got all mine.

I flip the phone book closed and slide it back under the telephone. After pulling on the backpack, I head for the door.

"How do we get there?" Reuben asks, following me.

"We take Birchwood to Gleason, turn on Waid, take that to Route 11, travel west to Factory Street, then onto Battle Hill Road. Then we just have to find his house. Shouldn't be hard."

"You sure he'll be there?"

"I can't be sure about anything." I open the door and walk down the porch steps. "And since I don't read minds, can't promise Jack will be anywhere. Just have to find him."

Reuben blinks his beady eyes. I turn away, unable look at him without staring like a creeper.

Reuben walks out of Jack and Noah's grandmother's house without closing the door behind him. I run back up the porch steps, twist the lock on the inside door handle, and close the door.

"What does it matter?" Reuben asks.

I shake my head and turn right. I start walking down Birchwood at a fast pace. We can probably make it to Jack's house by the end of the day as long as nothing unexpected occurs.

I turn left onto Waid Street. One of the dead is trapped inside a station wagon that's parked on the side of the road. The corpse inside is clawing at the windows as we walk by. The interior glass is coated with thick slime. Reuben stops to watch, his beak close to the glass of the driver's side window as the dead woman inside claws faster and snaps her teeth in rabid motion.

"Better hope that glass don't break," I warn. "Won't be liking yourself much, getting mauled by the dead." I shudder, remembering the stink of them.

Reuben backs away and continues following me.

We pass a sign for Route 11 when three of the dead take notice of us walking down the middle of the road. They amble toward us, moving faster than I expect. I grab my blade from the thigh holster. The weapon hums in my hand, seems to like being back on the plane from which it was forged. It cuts like butter through the necks of the dead. As the bodies drop, I glance at Reuben from the corner of my eye.

His beady eyes are blinking, his arms flap to the side. "Ca—caw!"

I startle. "What the hell was that for?"

"Stop looking at me, Meg."

"Of all the bullshit..." I start walking again, shaking my head in disgust.

There's a Price Chopper supermarket directly across the road from where we need to turn on Factory Street. I consider going inside. There's probably rows of Twinkies and snack crackers and shelf-stable chocolate milk in there. The last time I tried to enter a store on this plane it was already on lockdown by a group of the newly dead who almost shot my face off. I decide against going to the grocery store. It's best I avoid any traps that might prolong the search for Jack. The sooner I find him, the sooner I can be done with this. Snacks are tempting though.

I turn right and keep walking on the crumbling blacktop.

We make it about halfway to Battle Hill Road when my stomach grumbles loud and my backpack feels suddenly heavy. I hold my palms up and I notice my hands shaking. I'm beyond hungry, guess I've burned some calories these past few days.

"I have to stop for a minute," I warn Reuben.

I shrug off the backpack and search through the jars before deciding on one filled with corn and tomatoes.

"Do you have a fork?" I ask Reuben.

"Why would I have a fork?" His head tips to the side in question.

"I thought you'd be good for something." I twist open the jar, shake some of the corn and tomatoes inside into the lid, and eat off it.

"That smells good." Reuben steps closer and takes the jar out of my hand. He shoves his entire beak into the opening then he pulls the jar away and throws his head back, swallowing the corn and tomatoes with a strange gurgling noise.

"That was disgusting." I rip the jar out of his hand.

I stare into the divot made by his beak. I've eaten after worse. Once, when I was six, John Lewis hadn't cooked me dinner in nearly a week and I took an old peanut butter and jelly sandwich out of the local trailer park dog's mouth and ate it. Didn't even catch rabies, and I was certain that dog was afflicted. If I survived that I can survive eating after Reuben. These days my standards keep lowering and lowering.

I pour more of the corn mixture into the lid and throw it back.

Reuben holds his hand out expectantly.

"No."

"I'm hungry."

"Don't care," I reply as I chew.

"You have to feed me."

I walk away. "I don't have to do nothing."

The shackle around my neck constricts. I stop in my tracks, and turn to see Reuben's fist in the air, his fingers slowly opening and as they do the shackle around my neck loosens further. It loosens enough that I can finally swallow.

"Feed me," he demands.

I throw the jar at him.

Reuben catches it midair. I wasn't expecting that. The guy has fast reflexes for having that ridiculous crow head on top of his shoulders. I was expecting the beady eyes to impact his vision.

"I hope you choke on it," I say as I turn and start walking down the road.

Listening to Reuben eat is just as strange as watching. There are awkward gurgling noises as he tips his head back and swallows down the food without chewing.

The sun is starting to set and as the sky goes dark, thuds echo from all around us as the dead drop and sleep. I zip my jacket as the chill of the night seeps into my bones. There's a full moon illuminating the road.

The breaking of glass echoes.

I turn and see that Reuben has tossed the empty jar on the side of the road.

"Was that necessary?"

"Who cares?" He shrugs.

I press my lips together, hold in the kind of words that might get the shackle tightened around my neck again.

———

Sparrow

The scent of Hell was rich, thick, and pungent. Sparrow was sure he'd never forget it in all his life. He could barely remember the crispness of Heaven these days. That string that tethered his soul to the light was shredding, slowly. Sparrow was unsure what would happen to him when the last thread was plucked. If it was plucked. Maybe it would be the only bit left of who he used to be. Would he forget the origin of his soul? Would he forget *what* he used to be? He had Archangel blood running through his veins, and the mystic aura of Meg, ever since he'd fed from her that last time, just before she fled Hell to the earthen plane and when he visited her on the Earthen plane.

She'd changed him, just as Sparrow knew she would. He knew it the moment she was born, the first time he'd laid eyes on her. That was why he bolted and left her alone all those years to grow under the loathsome eye of John Lewis. The events that occurred afterward were inevitable; Sparrow couldn't escape this fate unscathed and neither could Meg, no matter how far she ran from him.

Sparrow focused out the expansive window that displayed the plane of Hell in all of its glory. Heat was rising from the land, shifting in waves like pavement on a hot summer day. Birds soared through the thickness of Hellsky. The leather of his wings ached to be stretched. Since taking Vine's place to the right hand of Lucifer, Sparrow spent much less time in the field. He had trained the newest set of Hellions, taught them to do things that would make the old Sparrow shudder in disgust. But he had to. He had to complete this and cure his family of the curse, it was the only way.

"Father!" Clea had come running into the room and

stopped at Lucifer's elbow. "She's back..." Clea had lowered her voice so that Sparrow couldn't hear the rest of the conversation. But he didn't miss the way Lucifer's massive, black wings stretched around her to give them privacy.

The fallen Angel was giant, taller than any Archangel Sparrow had ever met. And intimidating. But then, the ruler of Hell must have a certain way about him. There was only one chink in his armor. Sparrow had taken note of the way the King of Hell changed when the spirit of his daughter was near. He'd have to be dumb and blind to miss it. The winged-devil was an ink stain from the Heavens, dark and foreboding, but when Clea was near it was almost as if he had a small blooming daisy sticking out of the front pocket of his leather vest, bright and unexpected.

Sparrow knew better, there was nothing bright about Lucifer, just a deep, dark, smudge of a soul; a giant black hole that ebbed with power and threatened to absorb and demolish anything that came near.

Lucifer's wings snapped open and came to rest tight against his back. Clea fled the room, a soul on a mission. Sparrow waited in silence, forced his curiosity down and away. His face revealed not a speck of interest.

Lucifer leaned back in his chair, propped colossal black boots on the top of the desk, wove his fingers behind his scalp, and focused on the twenty-foot stone ceiling. Sparrow was sure something was writhing in the shadows up there, some pet of Lucifer's, but he had yet to see it, only heard the whisper of tough skin sliding against stone. It was a frequent focus of Lucifer, which led Sparrow to believe that something was up there.

"Son," Lucifer called.

Sparrow cringed inwardly, keeping his face stone solid. Lucifer refused to call Sparrow by his given name, even suggested he change it to something else. When Sparrow refused the King of Hell began referring to him as *son* in private. Sparrow knew he was no son of Lucifer, he was a son of the Archangel Remiel. Sparrow was born of light and good; he would never be a son of Lucifer, no matter how dark this time in Hell turned his soul.

"Sir," Sparrow replied.

Lucifer never took his eyes off of the shadowed ceiling. "We have a problem to the North. The Deacons are pulling some shit again. I need you to go stop them."

Sparrow crossed the room, stopped for a moment and turned. "Are there more details?"

Lucifer smiled, his thin lips spreading in a line. "Where's the fun in giving you details?"

Sparrow waited for a moment before Lucifer waved him away.

He made his way out of Lucifer's office, walked the few hundred yards to the stairwell then ran up three steps at a time. As he reached the landing to the main floor, Clea appeared, nearly transparent, nearly a dark twin of the only woman Sparrow had ever loved in his entire life. Sparrow slowed his pace, focused on her mouth, which was moving but no sound came out. Sparrow focused on the way her lips pressed together and, without a doubt, she mouthed "*Meg*" at him. Clea couldn't give him a verbal hint within range of Lucifer, he'd hear and then both of them would pay.

Lucifer wanted Sparrow to be surprised.

Clea wanted swift action.

A low growl began in Sparrow's throat. Clea disappeared as

Sparrow ran down the hall, past the Hellion lair, his boots muted by eons-old Persian rugs covering the stone floor. He made it to the mouth of the cave, a cloud of dirt swirling around Sparrow's feet as heavy boots landed just before he launched himself into the air, spread the leather wings that had replaced his feathered white ones when he gave his soul to the devil, and took off into the evening sky.

Sparrow flew north as fast as he could. Before he'd made it far from the burning caves of Hell the Argentavis was at his side. Clea had joined him, which told Sparrow all he needed to know. The daughter of Lucifer never hesitated for a moment when it came to her own child.

Meg was in Hell and she was in trouble. Clea would know exactly where she was.

Sparrow flew faster.

Meg

A shadow passes over the road in front of me, it blocks out the moonlight for a few moments. A second one joins it. The shadows circle, like there's some giant bird in the air threatening to land, with a friend by its side. My heart skips a few beats at the hope of Clea returning to help get me out of this mess.

"Don't look up," Reuben warns.

Of course I immediately tilt my head up only to have it forced back down. I can't help it. Anyone else would do the same.

We walk and the shadows circle continuously until we reach Battle Hill Road, then they disappear.

"What was that?" I ask as I take a left.

"It's best you don't know."

"Maybe I'd like to know."

"Too bad for you."

"What does it matter if I know?"

"The less distractions the better. There are a lot of souls on the table. You need to find Jack."

"I'll find fucking Jack," I mutter under my breath.

We walk down the empty road, moonlight turning the path sepia, until we get to the mailbox labeled "Jack Cooper."

The farmhouse is small with a wraparound porch painted green, an American flag hanging, tattered and soiled. You have to know you're in Hell when you come across a north country house with the flag still hanging at night, looking like that. We may not have our teeth or a positive balance in our bank account, but we know better than to leave our country's flag hanging out at night. Jack would never do that.

I step up onto the porch and try the door handle. It's unlocked. I push the door open as I search my pack for a flashlight.

"Jack?" I call. I flick the flashlight on. The light illuminates wedding pictures of Jack and Charlotte. They looked happy on their wedding day at least. But, Charlotte wasn't smiling like that when I met her at the hospital and she didn't sound as happy as she looks in this picture. It seems time stretches all relationships.

Everything is faded, dirty and dank; the house smells musty. This is the dark reflection of the Earthen plane. I imagine their real house to be light and airy.

I search the living room, kitchen, dining room; every nook and cranny, but Jack's house is empty. I stop in the master bedroom, take a glance at the neatly made queen sized bed. Exhaustion hits. I haven't had a good night's rest in days. I crawl into Jack and Charlotte's bed and fall asleep.

I dream of Sparrow... *He's come to rescue me, kicked the front door of Jack's house open and chopped Reuben into tiny bits. Little black feathers from Reuben's head litter the air; Sparrow walks through them like a God returning home from war; intent, muscles rippling. My mouth waters anticipating the sweet taste of his blood on my tongue. My skin pebbles with gooseflesh awaiting the feel of his hands. He bends to join me on the bed, his lips parting, knees pressing into the mattress, his tongue snakes out and he licks my cheek. Something isn't right, Sparrow smells like rotting flesh. When my hands touch his skin, he's no longer firm and muscular but soft and decaying.*

My eyes flash open and I find one of the rotting flesh-bags snapping its gums at me.

I scream before lifting my knees and kicking the thing off me. The dead man stumbles and falls on his back. I grab my blade and slice it's head off. I wipe my arm across my face to remove the slime and ichor.

There's a chuckle from the doorway.

Reuben is standing there. "I was wondering when you were going to wake up."

"You're worthless." I pick up my bag, leave the room, and find a new place to sleep. The spare room has a walk-in closet. I lock myself inside and curl up on the floor.

Sparrow

There was an invisible force propelling Sparrow away from the farmhouse in front of him.

"I can't get near it," Sparrow growled as he took a step forward. It felt like he was trying to walk through drying concrete.

A cool hand settled on his bare shoulder. "You should conserve your energy."

Sparrow stepped back. "It's the Scarecrow." He shook his head. "It's stronger than the first time I came across it."

"We have to find a way around it." Clea sat on the ground, her gown settling around her in soft layers. "The longer it is with her, the stronger it will become."

Sparrow joined her, the leather of his pants stretching tight against his thighs as he sat cross-legged. His mouth watered, it had been over a week since he last fed from Meg. Knowing that she was so close and that he couldn't have her burned, made his gut ache and twist. He'd have to go back to the Hellion lair for bagged blood. He wouldn't be at his strongest but he couldn't allow himself to get weak. Not with her here.

"You should go back," Clea whispered. "I'll wait with her."

Sparrow stood, didn't want to leave but knew he had to. He'd be back within a few hours, at the most.

"Go," Clea shooed him. "Before she wakes and they start traveling again."

Sparrow bent his knees and in one powerful movement he launched himself into the air, circled the farmhouse twice, and then headed back to the burning caves. But, before he left, he didn't miss the way Clea settled her chin on folded hands and narrowed her gaze on the farmhouse.

Meg

I wake to dull thudding against the closet door. Sitting up quick, I reach for my blade and peer through the slats. There's a shadow aimlessly wandering the room. Where the heck is Reuben? I shove the closet door open, relieve the walking sack-o-flesh of its head, then turn to pick up my bag. I leave the room, cursing myself. I searched this entire house last night. Granted, I only had a flashlight, but the shadows of Hell can only hide so much. I wouldn't expect to miss two of the dead, not when they smell like they do. My game must be off. I lick my lips. Or maybe I'm hungry for more than canned goods.

I head down the stairs, stopping when I see the open back door. Goddamn Reuben. The guy is worthless.

Glancing through the window, I see Reuben in the backyard pecking at the ground. He pulls an early morning worm from the dirt, tosses his head back and swallows it down. Bile rises in the back of my throat. I've never been so disgusted by another person, but watching old Crow-head is more disturbing than trying to come to terms with how much I enjoy the taste of blood.

I kick the door closed and sit at the breakfast bar. The way I see it, Jack has two choices. He goes to find his estranged wife or he goes to find more protection and maybe even a working car. Since he's law enforcement, I bet he's going to work, that's what they always to in the movies. Which means we must backtrack. The trooper barracks are near the jail that I broke out of when I first woke up here.

I glance out the window again. Reuben's really going at it

with the worms. While he's filling his gut, I take the moment to eat in peace. I open the backpack and pull out another jar. This one is filled with some kind of canned meat. I get up and search for some silverware in Jack's cupboards. There's a whole bunch of silverware in a drawer next to the sink. I take one for now and a few spoons for the road. I sit down again and dig in. The meat tastes like deer. I never knew Jack and Noah's grandma to be a hunter. Maybe their grandfather caught it and she canned it before he died? That would have been years ago. I take another mouthful and decide it doesn't taste rotten. So I eat the entire jar, and then hide the evidence in a cupboard so Reuben doesn't see. I don't want him asking for more of my food.

I shoulder my pack and walk out the back door. Reuben is standing still as a statue, staring into the surrounding forest.

"What are you looking at?" I ask.

Reuben makes a throaty noise. "Ca—caw!" There's rustling from the forest, an *umph*, like a man fell over. Maybe he scared one of the walking dead?

That noise he makes is really annoying.

"I think we should get moving," I suggest.

I head for the road. Reuben follows. I wonder how his gut feels being full of worms? Do they slither and slide around in there or are they immediately put to rest by the gastric juices? I shudder, glad that I don't require a steady diet of worms to keep going. But, thinking about my lack of supplies and dwindling time, searching for bugs in the dirt like some survivalist on a TV show might become my new reality. I hope to hell not.

We head for the trooper barracks, keeping a fast enough pace that the dead don't catch up with us. Now that the haze from Raguel's beating has passed, I feel pretty good. I've got a full stomach and I slept like a rock last night, if not for that dream of Sparrow and having to chop off that dead man's head. To think of it, that's the first dream I've had in a while—that didn't include my teeth falling out of my head.

"I used to dream of a friend. Haven't heard from her in a while."

Reuben chuckles. "Not while I'm around."

I narrow my gaze on him. "Why?"

"I filter all distractions. That includes Sparrow, and that includes visitors in dreams, and that includes any of the newly dead, besides Jack."

"And those rotting sacks of flesh?"

"What about them?" Reuben shrugs and blinks his beady eyes. "You're doing a fine job taking care of them yourself."

God, he really is worthless. I turn and walk faster, before I can remove one of his Chucks and shove it down his gullet.

I take a left on Factory Street and scratch at the shackle around my neck. My skin is sore from where it rubbed in the night. I hate that I have to backtrack to the trooper barracks. Hate even more that I must set eyes on that jail again. But, growing up here one learns shortcuts, and I know that if I cut through this few acres of woods and go off road, they'll open up exactly where we need to be. I step off the road, make my way down the embankment, hop across the ditch, and march into the cover of the forest.

The shackle tightens around my neck. "Where are you going?" Reuben asks.

"Taking the scenic route." My fingers tug at the metal cutting into my skin.

"I'm not going to tolerate your trickery." He sounds annoyed.

"For the tune of four hundred souls I think you'll tolerate a lot." I take another step; the shackle cuts off my air supply. I gasp, claw, scratch the skin of my neck raw, until it finally releases.

"Don't forget, Meg, I read your files, memorized it while I was preparing for your trial. Jailbait like you are always up to no good."

I come to the conclusion that Reuben is a complete jackass.

I lead him through the trees, the snapping of twigs and rustling of dead leaves under my boots worry me that the dead will come looking for the noise. Fortunately we exit the cover of the trees and step onto the narrow unnamed road that leads to the trooper barracks.

"See?" I point so Reuben can see that I wasn't pulling one on him, just trying to make my life a bit easier for a few minutes.

"We've got company," is all he says.

A cruiser is speeding down the road, headed away from the jail. I move to the side of the road. The driver glances, does a double take, then slams on the brakes. He nearly leaps from the cruiser, gun in hand.

It's Jack.

"Meg?" He rounds the vehicle. "Meg! Oh God, is that really you?"

"It's me, Jack." I stand still, let him take it all in.

"What the hell..." He's getting an eyeful of my odd companion. "What the fuck is *that*?" Jack aims his gun at Reuben's bird head.

I pause, wondering what will happen if Jack blasts Reuben's dome off. Maybe I'll be free of him?

"You'll go straight back to that cell in Babylon." Reuben breaks the moment of silence. "If I die, you go straight back,

Meg. You don't stop at go, you don't get two hundred dollars, you go straight to jail."

Shit.

Jack's face is twisted in disgust as he watches the talking birdman.

"Jack?" I take a few steps toward him, hands up in surrender. "Jack. We need to talk."

"What *is* that?" His finger tenses against the trigger of his handgun.

Jack looks so much like his younger brother Noah. I can't take my eyes off him.

"Jack! You need to focus." I wave at Reuben and walk closer to Jack. "Forget Reuben, forget that he has the... the head of a crow—"

Jack fires off four shots. My gut sinks. I squeeze my eyes closed, anticipating that feeling, the gutless dizziness of traveling between realms as I'm dragged back to Babylon.

It never comes.

A warm hand grabs mine. "We have to get out of here," Jack says.

My eyes flick open. I turn to see four of the dead laying in the road and Reuben standing there, very much alive and still breathing.

"Is that some kind of a mask?" Jack asks as he tugs me toward the passenger side of the cruiser.

"Not really." I get in and close the door.

Reuben starts walking and gets in the back seat as Jack makes his way to the driver's side. I take my pack off and set it at my feet. Doors slam. Jack starts the cruiser, glancing at Reuben in the back.

I don't trust him behind me, but at least there's the cage

separating us and I don't have to worry about Reuben's beak stabbing me in the back of the head if shit goes bad.

"I can't believe this is happening." Jack puts the cruiser into gear and presses his foot down on the gas. I'm not sure how much horsepower a Crown Victoria has, but it's enough to sandwich me to my seat. Jack takes the country roads faster than I ever have sober and in the daylight.

"All these dead things walking around. I–I must've killed fifteen of them, at least." He wipes his hand across his mouth, "I just can't believe it. Watched all those zombie shows as a kid but never expected that it could actually happen."

Jack finally slows the Crown Vic.; there's a large group of the dead walking across the road ahead of us. I adjust my seatbelt and face him.

"Explain it to me." Jack is scowling as he focuses on the road, weaving around the herd. "Explain these dead people walking around."

"What's the last thing you remember?" I ask.

Jack presses his lips together in thought for a moment. "I was at work. Night shift. I was patrolling alone. Pulled some Jeep over for speeding on the back roads. Deer were heavy that night, nearly hit three myself." Jack slows his speed. "I got out of the car... and..."

Silence.

"And what?" I ask.

"I can't remember." Jack shakes his head. "I just know that I woke up in a hospital, a tube down my throat choking me. I pulled everything out. Ran out of the hospital half naked." He's shaking his head from side to side. "This is just... *messed* up, Meg."

I swallow hard, getting ready to lay the truth on him.

"This is like those TV shows everyone was watching. All these dead people walking about, trying to eat your face off."

"Jack—"

"I mean," he laughs, "I *never* thought this could ever happen. Knew our country was headed to the toilet but this. This!"

"Jack—"

"And I can't find one person I know. Well, besides you, you're the first live person I've found. For a while there I thought I was the only one. All alone. I thought—"

"Jack!"

He pauses. "What?"

"You're in Hell."

Rubber squeals on dry pavement as Jack slams on the brakes.

He turns to me, paler than when I saw him on life support in the hospital.

I break all the rules and touch him, lay my hand on his upper arm. "Jack. Listen to me. This is going to sound crazy but... you died. Something happened and you died and you're in Hell because you killed John Lewis."

"Your father?"

"Yes. No. Kind of. He wasn't my real father." I squeeze his arm. "It doesn't matter. What matters is that we have to get you out of here. You deserve better than Hell. We have to get you to a Safe House so you can repent."

"Repent?"

"Yes. So you'll go to Heaven."

"What's a Safe House?" Jack asks.

"It's like a prison. They're prisons on the earthen plane but here they are a safe place where you can be protected."

Jack gets a faraway look in his eyes. "I died."

"I'm sorry, but you died. You're dead."

"I feel alive." He pats his chest. "I can't be dead. I feel so *alive*."

"It's another kind of life. Another plane. But if we don't get you help one day you'll wake up like them." I point to the walking sacks of flesh ambling past the cruiser.

Jack glances in the rearview mirror.

"She's telling the truth," Reuben says. His beak opens and closes as he speaks. Without lips I wonder how he forms the words so clearly.

Jack glances at me.

"It's going to take a while to explain that," I thumb toward the back seat, "to you." I remove my hand from Jack's arm. "You need to drive." I turn in my seat to ask Reuben, "Where's the closest Safe House?"

"Kingston or Auburn." Reuben folds his hands in his lap. "Pick one."

I can't go to Kingston. Not after that trek with Sparrow. Every step will be a memory.

"Auburn," I say.

"I think Kingston is closer," Jack argues.

"We should go to Auburn," I say.

"Thirty minute difference," birdman says.

"Auburn. I can't go to Kingston."

"Why?" Jack asks.

"Bad memories."

"Noah died on his way to Auburn Correctional." Jack's tone is flat.

Silence.

"There are other correctional facilities. Ogdensburg,

Franklin County, Chateaugay, Adirondack." Jack's counting on his fingers as he lists them. "Altona, Washington, Great Meadow, Midstate, Mohawk."

I turn to look at Reuben. "All those other places and you didn't tell me."

Crowhead shrugs like he could care less.

"Which one is closest?" I ask Jack.

"Franklin."

"Just because it's close doesn't mean it's safe," Reuben interrupts, "doesn't mean it's taking new stragglers. Some are full. Some are overrun with the dead. Some are a treacherous journey through the land of Hell. Auburn or Kingston. Those are your choices."

"Fine." Jack gives up. "Auburn."

"*Thank you*," I whisper.

"We'll have to drive some back roads. Route 11 through town is clogged with cars and those things." He points at a dead man walking by, his button-down shirt torn to tattered rags. "We can hit the highway in Adams Center."

SPARROW

Sparrow fed, nearly used all the stock from the fridge in the lair, but he needed to ensure strength. Even though his beast was sated, that hollow depth in his soul still crooned for Meg. Having her within the same realm was nearly unbearable. At least with her on the Earthen plane the ache was nothing more than an incessant buzzing that he could ignore, mostly.

Sparrow crossed the lair, stepped out into the stone hallway and closed the door behind him. He remembered a time when the Hellion lair was his home. As short of a time as it was, it was a time he'd never forget. Nearly all his memories had returned, the moments in which Jim and Vine died, it was all released, slammed into his skull so hard he could barely think. He could hardly process the situation between him and Meg. The moment he was promoted to Lucifer's first in command, the moment Meg asked *"Do you remember?"* and then she flashed away to the earthen plane.

"There's a newly dead uprising in Chicago. It's a religious cult. They're trying to summon greater demons from below," Skeele, the newly appointed leader of the Hellions interrupted Sparrow's thoughts.

"Send a crew to take care of it."

"Sir?"

Sparrow turned. The large Hellion standing in front of him could always sense when Sparrow was distracted.

"Is there more?" Sparrow asked.

Skeele was tame at the moment, all business, but Sparrow had seen the Hellion at his worst, in full battle mode with not a rational bone in his body. Together they had shaped the Hellions to be more than brute strength and evil.

"There are rumors that we have visitors," Skeele finally said.

Many knew about Meg. But they needed to subdue the chatter. If the newly dead learned that a drop of Meg's blood would let them crawl out of Hell, she'd be in more danger than she already was. Sparrow cursed, he was hoping to keep her return to Hell a secret. She was headstrong, that was a part of her that would never change, but Sparrow wished for one second that she'd consider her safety. This was a bad situation overall. He couldn't get near her, which meant he couldn't protect her. Sparrow didn't like it one bit.

It wasn't so long ago that the last batch of Hellions conspired against Lucifer, creating an unsanctioned portal and using Meg's blood to cross between realms. They were all dead now. But Lucifer wasn't quick to trust. He held Sparrow's freedom in a vice grip. And while Sparrow was only promised a short duration as a Hellion to free his family from its curse, he was not certain what Lucifer's definition of short was.

"Quell the rumors," Sparrow instructed. "Keep everyone away from her and the Scarecrow."

"Despicable vermin." Skeele's lips peel back, revealing sharp teeth. "They should be wiped from all realms."

"I will watch her." Sparrow moved for the door.

"And if Lucifer calls on you?"

"You will watch her. But keep your distance," Sparrow warned. "Her history with the Hellions has been fouled. She'd sooner cut your head off than let you get close enough to touch her."

Skeele nodded. "Noted."

Sparrow left the burning caves. He stretched his wings, flying fast. When he reached the farmhouse, everyone was gone.

Meg

"Please tell me you've got some supplies in this thing." I pat the armrest.

Jack glances at me. "The trunk's full of ammo. I took everything from work. Emptied out the snack machines too. There wasn't much, though. Not sure how long this is going to last."

"We just need to get to Auburn. Just need to make it through today." Knowing that he has some food is calming. I don't want to lose control from hunger.

Jack leans forward and taps on the gas gauge. "Hopefully there's enough to make it."

My stomach growls.

"You hungry, Meg?" Jack asks. "I can pull over and get some stuff out of the trunk."

I glance at him, noticing his jugular throbbing. I'm fixated on it. Saliva pools in my mouth.

Jack looks at me. "What's that thing around your neck?" he asks.

I snap out of it and touch the shackle. "Ask him." I thumb toward the backseat.

Jack checks out Reuben in the rearview mirror. "So?"

"To keep her on task," Reuben says.

"I think you should take it off."

"Can't do that."

"I think you should. It's demeaning. Take it off."

"It might come in handy. You may thank me for having control over her."

Jack glances at me. "What's he talking about?"

"Just... drive. I'll explain later."

For the first time, Jack looks uneasy around me. I'll never explain my blood thirst to him. I can barely deal with it myself. Sparrow, Nightingale and my mother are the only ones who know, so far. Jack doesn't need to know. It will only make him wary of me. And I can't have that, there are things I need him to do.

WE'RE ON ROUTE 81, headed south. We stop for a bathroom break at one of the highway rest stops. There are no paper towels in the women's rest room. I guess there's no one stocking and cleaning. I dry my hands on my filthy jeans as I'm walking out of the reststop.

"Why haven't I seen other people?" Jack asks as I'm walking toward the car. "Just you, and... him."

"Reuben is blocking them," I reply. "We're on a mission to get you to Heaven. No distractions."

"Why?" Jack asks, suddenly somber. "Why does it matter if I go to Heaven or stay here in Hell?"

"Jack," I touch his arm, "you don't deserve Hell."

"And if you don't repent, Meg goes back to jail," Reuben adds. "Meg thinks she doesn't deserve jail."

"Shut your stupid mouth," I warn Reuben. No one deserves that jail in Heaven.

Jack knows my past, he barely seems surprised. "Spill it, Meg. Tell me everything. Now."

"Jack, it's too much." I advance on Reuben, grab the blade from my thigh holster. The shackle tightens, so tight.

"Tell him, Meg. Tell him what a mess you've gotten yourself into," Reuben prods.

"When this is done, I'm going to take great joy gutting you like a pig."

Reuben jerks his fist closed and I drop to the ground, wheezing and gasping.

"Let her go!" Jack is yelling at Reuben but it sounds so far away. I hear the click of Jack's handgun.

The shackle finally loosens. I lay on the ground, stars

occluding my vision, my throat burning, mouth dry as I take deep breaths.

A shadow passes over us, something falls from the sky. At first it's a speck, then it gets closer, and closer, and closer. It's a book. I roll just before it smacks me in the face. The book falls with a thud, the spine hits the ground and bounces the book onto its side. I crawl on my knees to the book. It's Sparrow's hardcover, *Birds of Paradise*. Just as I'm reaching for it, Reuben kicks the book. It rolls across the parking lot, stopping at Jack's feet.

Jack bends and picks it up.

Reuben walks away.

"What's this?" Jack asks as he unfolds the torn and bent pages.

I move to my feet and take the book. "A message," I search the sky but find no one flying about, "hopefully."

It looks about the same, a little more damaged now that it's fallen from the sky and been kicked. I flip through the pages, stopping when I notice handwriting in the margin.

> *Darkness becomes,*
> *Darkness it stays,*
> *Sparrow is coming for you,*
> *He's been trying for days.*

WELL, that's subtle. Since I've never seen Sparrow or Clea's handwriting, I'm not sure who left the note, and if it was Sparrow, why does he refer to himself in the third person?

"Who's Sparrow?" Jack asks.

I close the book and start heading for the cruiser. "Sparrow is... complicated."

Jack follows and we both get in the cruiser. Reuben's already in the back seat. I swallow hard, ignore the soreness in my throat, and do my best to ignore him as well.

Jack starts the cruiser and drives out of the rest area. We head south, taking the exit for the thruway.

"So," Jack clears his throat, "this Sparrow guy?"

I do my best to explain Sparrow and our relationship. And as I'm nearing the end, having avoided any suspect details, Reuben's beak makes an appearance between us as he leans forward from the backseat. "Did you tell him you're the granddaughter of Lucifer?"

Jack slows his speed. "Always thought you were a bit dark, Meg. But that's stuff they put in the movies. It's kinda hard wrapping my head around all of this."

"I think you're doing a good job of it." I say as I tuck *Birds of Paradise* between the seat and the center console for safekeeping.

"Why don't you ask her about Noah?" Reuben suggests.

"What about Noah?" Jack's eyes narrow on me.

"He was here, in Hell." I take a deep breath, knowing that Jack probably doesn't want to hear this about his little brother. "He didn't repent. Lucifer owns his soul."

"Don't stop now, Meg," Reuben squawks. "Spill the beans."

I close my eyes, remembering the moments in which he went from one of my best friends to a walking sack of flesh. I tell Jack how it happened. There is only silence as Jack is informed of his brother never leaving the realm of Hell.

"So where's Noah now?" Jack asks.

"I'm pretty sure he's in the Astral plane."

This leads to other conversations about ethereal realms and traveling souls. By the time the conversation is over Jack looks exhausted. I still didn't tell him about the whole blood-sucking part though. I don't need Jack's judgment.

Jack turns on to route 34 and follows the road into Auburn. There are signs on the side of the road here, just like in Kingston. Instructions to wait in designated places for transport to the Safe House. No one's waiting, though. I don't even see a bus similar to the one that picked us up. It could be here and I'm blind to it, due to the jerk with a bird head in the backseat.

I wonder what else is going on around us that I can't see? I guess it's not so bad, having those things blocked out. I went nearly twenty-five years on the Earthen plane having Heaven and Hell and the creatures inhabited by both realms invisible to me. I guess it does help a person focus. Still, it's strange how these ethereal beings can alter someone's perspective. On the Earthen plane their attributions to what realm they belong to are hidden; those poor people must go off character alone. I glance at Reuben. It didn't work too well for me. I was still fooled.

THE AUBURN safe house isn't much different from the Kingston Safe House; miles of chain-link fence topped with barbed wire, guards pacing with weapons in hand. One walks toward the gate, keys jingling. I feel suddenly nervous, palms sweaty and heart pumping.

"Scarecrow," the guard greets birdhead. His eyes narrow on

me then Jack. "You can come in for the Qualifiers. You leave for the Quarantine. We already know you won't be repenting." Keys clank together as the guard unlocks and opens the gate.

They collect our bags and weapons. A guard motions to the blade strapped to my thigh.

"Not a sinner's chance in Hell, buddy." I cross my arms.

That damn shackle tightens. "Give it up, Meg," Reuben warns.

I unstrap the leather and hand it over, all the while imagining the variety of ways in which I'm going to expire Reuben's life.

We sit at a table.

A guard hands Jack two pieces of paper and a pen.

"What's this?" Jack asks.

"Your Qualifier," I say. "Just fill it out. A Deacon will review it."

Jack fills in the blanks for his name, date of birth, and every other personally identifying tidbit about himself. Wasn't so long ago that I did the same thing. That was before I knew what I was.

Jack flips to the second page. *Are you searching for someone?*

"Am I?" Jack asks.

"Are you?" I ask.

He writes *Noah*.

I've already told Jack about Noah, and the slim likelihood of him seeing his brother ever again. Our goal is to get Jack to Heaven, and Noah can't go there, the devil owns his soul. Highly doubt it's ever gonna happen.

What is your greatest sin? Is the next question.

Jack glances at me.

"What?"

"I'm no boyscout."

I never expected Jack to be trooper of the year, but the things he writes down on that paper make me reconsider the pedestal I've put the man on. Besides murder, there was a bit of theft, a little racketeering, gambling, some heavy drinking, and infidelity.

The pen clicks, he flips the papers over. "What's next?"

"We wait for the Deacon. His name will be Deacon."

"That's not confusing."

"Yup." I look at Jack, unable to forget all the sins he wrote down on that paper.

"Don't look at me like that." Jack crosses his arms and leans back in his chair.

"I just wasn't expecting—"

"Nobody's perfect."

Well, he's got that right.

Footsteps echo and the door opens. The Deacon shows. "Jack," he holds out a hand to greet Jack. They shake. "My name's Deacon. We've been expecting you." He sits across from Jack and reviews the papers. "I will be your Parole Officer. I'm responsible for locating your loved one and helping you through the Quarantine process." Deacon scans the first sheet of paper. "Unfortunately, I won't be able to locate your brother. Is there anyone else?"

"No." Jack shakes his head.

The Deacon glances at me. "Since there's no one else, and she can't enter here, we can't release you to the general population."

"What's that mean?"

"You'll stay in your cell. Alone."

Jack glances at me. Being confined to a cell for more than

twenty-four hours is pretty crappy. I smile, hoping he doesn't back out.

The Deacon clears his throat. "The next step is showing you to your cell."

I know what's in store for him next, a set of maroon scrubs known as Newcomer uniforms, a barren cell, a slew of interviews by the men who sit behind the desk-of-questioning. I'm not really sure what happens after that. I didn't stick around long enough to experience it when I was here myself.

"Would you like something to eat?" Deacon asks Jack as they stand.

"Yes." Jack doesn't hesitate one second.

They start walking away. Jack pauses, he turns and makes his way toward me. "I'll see you on the other side." He says as he crushes me in a tight hug.

Jack lets go and returns to the Deacon's side.

I sure hope so, I think.

The cry of metal on metal fills the room as a guard opens the door leading to the cells. Jack steps through, following Deacon, the door slams, and then it's just me and Reuben.

His beak opens. "Ca—caw!"

I punch him in the face.

Suicide Party

I'M SITTING on a cement block on the edge of the parking lot. Reuben's off in a field hunting worms. I'm trying to figure out how he's going to retaliate for me punching him in his stupid face. I keep swallowing, expecting the shackle to tighten at any moment. But nothing happens. Reuben gets further and further away from me.

The guards at the Safe House gave me back my blade. I wasn't expecting that. Last time I was at one of these places they kept my guns upon release. I hop down from the cement block and head toward Jack's car. I pop the trunk and rummage through the bag of snacks, taking a bag of chips, a candy bar, and a soda. I slam the trunk closed and walk around the car, sitting in the passenger side, and eat.

I wonder how safe we are here and how long before they'll release Jack. I try to think back on the few things I knew about the bible, but I curse myself for not doing some research during all of this.

I pull *Birds of Paradise* from between the seat and center console and open it. The pages crinkle, stuck together from me dropping food between the pages months ago when I was trapped in my room in Hell and bored to death. There's pizza sauce, syrup, and crumbs that fall into my lap as I turn the pages and glance at the birds.

I wonder how many Hail Marys they're making Jack recite? There wasn't much redemption for me when I sought out a Safe House. They said they couldn't help me because Jim didn't show up to collect me. They kept me locked up and only released me to bring me to the questioning sessions with those old men sitting at that table.

"You have that look in your eyes," the one on the left says.
"What look is that?" I ask.
"Like you've almost lost all hope."

A YELLOW FINCH lands on the hood of the cruiser. It chirps a short trill before flying through the air, bouncy and rolling in some strange dance with the wind. I wonder what it would be like to fly as free as that finch.

The snacks are gone much too soon. My stomach is still grumbling. I recline the passenger seat, prop my feet up on the dash, close my eyes, and dream of Heaven fare. The food up there was delicious, well, before they locked me up and beat me.

I've got nothing to do while I wait for Jack. I roll up the windows to the cruiser, lock all the doors and curl in the seat for a nap.

Sparrow

Sparrow was walking with determination, headed to his quarters to change his clothes and collect his blade. He'd been unable to locate Meg. Skeele had captured a Deacon and beat some information out of him. Meg was headed for a safe house, but the Deacon didn't know which one. Sparrow had searched the Safe Houses, starting with the one in Kingston; he wasn't sure which one she was headed to. But he hadn't felt that force near any of the Safe Houses he'd been to, that force which shoved him away from her.

After changing into something clean, Sparrow collected his blade and left his quarters.

Lucifer appeared in the center of the hall, blocking him.

"Sir?" Sparrow asked.

"Are you up to no good, son?" Lucifer asked.

Sparrow was silent. He was so intent on going after Meg that he hadn't prepared an excuse for what he was doing.

"Did the Hellions take care of the religious uprising in Chicago?"

"Yes." Sparrow tipped his head. "All settled. Now, I must see to a disturbance near one of the Safe Houses."

Lucifer stood to the side. "My daughter has told me that Meg has returned to Hell."

Sparrow stilled. "I've heard the same."

"Have you seen her?" Lucifer asked.

"Yes, sir."

"Do not forget that you are my right hand."

Sparrow had been promoted after he and Gabriel decimated the previous group of Hellions, killing them all, their commander and Lucifer's first in charge. Even though a betrayal of epic proportions was revealed, Lucifer made Sparrow pay for the deaths by extending his term as a Hellion. His time was already longer than any of the Archangels or their children had spent in Hell. But Sparrow couldn't leave; he had to relieve his bloodline of the curse.

Sparrow bowed. "I will not, sir."

Lucifer motioned for Sparrow to carry on.

Sparrow knew he had to tread lightly. After the situation with Jim and Vine, Lucifer was checking up on everyone. That included Sparrow and the greater demons he had assigned as Hellions.

Clea and Skeele met him at the mouth of the burning caves.

"We've found her," Skeele said.

"Where?" Sparrow was ready to launch from where he stood to collect her.

"Calm down," Clea soothed. "She's carrying a bit of magic in her pocket that will help break the Scarecrow's hold. Give it time."

"Then we'll go together and get her now." Sparrow moved to leave but the cool hand of Clea stopped him.

"You can't storm a Safe House and you can't break the Scarecrow's stronghold alone. You must wait. Patience."

Sparrow paced. "We can't wait. This has been going on for long enough." His wings flexed in agitation. "I want her back. Now."

"You know storming a Safe House is a suicide mission." Skeele looked bored which annoyed Sparrow further. "Lucifer will have our hides mounted on his wall."

Clea interrupted them, "My father knows she's here. Organizing this against his wishes will result in consequences."

"I don't care," Sparrow said. "She is mine and this is dangerous. I will not allow her to be hurt further." Sparrow clenched his fists.

"I agree that you shouldn't be apart from her, the longer this goes on, the more vulnerable the ethereal realms become." Clea looked worried.

Suddenly Sparrow felt the tug from Lucifer. He was being called and it was impossible for him to deny the demand.

Sparrow looked at Skeele. "You go watch her. Do not leave her until I arrive."

Skeele took to the sky in the direction of the Auburn Safe House and Sparrow re-entered the burning caves to find out what Lucifer required of him this time.

MEG

Jack is walking the perimeter of the Safe House fence. It's nice of them to let him get some fresh air. I remember how stifling those cells can get.

I leave the cruiser where I've been shacked up for the past two days and run toward him. Jack looks gaunt and pale.

"Jack?" I grip the fencing.

He turns to me, dark circles under his eyes.

"What's going on in there?" I ask.

Jack is wearing the maroon Newcomer uniform, nothing but formless scrubs. His hands are in his pockets as he stares at me, searching for his words.

"Jack?" I rattle the fencing.

"You didn't tell me it would be like this," he finally says.

"Like what?" Last time I was in there, the worst part was the bitchy chick that was responsible for bringing me my meals.

He tilts his face to the sky. The days in Hell are anything but bright, but there is a sun and I know it's brighter than the light inside the Safe House.

Jack inhales a deep breath before he asks, "When you told them all the crap you did as a kid, what was your penance?"

"I didn't have any. I didn't repent. I left."

That day was both heartbreaking and freeing, realizing that Jim wasn't going to get me but being reunited with Sparrow again.

Jack looks surprised. "I'd like to leave then. I want out."

My heart sinks. If he leaves, I go back to that jail cell in Heaven, and Raguel's punishments. "You can't. Jack, you must atone. You don't belong here. You have to make it to Heaven. It's only been two days. Just, try a little longer. Please?"

Jack pulls his hands out of his pockets and holds them up to the fence so I can see the bright red slashes across the backs of his hands.

"What the..." It feels like a stone sinking in my gut.

"I was expecting to say some prayers, maybe pray on the rosary, recite the bible, but this," he shakes his head, "is not what I was anticipating."

"I didn't know." I should have known. I should have known a heck of a lot better after Raguel. "I'll talk to the Deacons. Just, wait here for me."

I run to the front gate. When I glance back at Jack, he's wandering the perimeter of the yard again.

"Let me in," I demand of a guard.

He looks down at me.

"Now. I need to speak with a Deacon."

The guard jingles his keys, taking his time opening the gate and letting me inside. I follow the guard inside to the same place where Jack filled out his Qualifier paperwork.

The guard reaches for my blade.

"I don't think so, buddy." I step away from him. "Get me a Deacon." I grip the hilt of my blade.

The guard walks to the door and speaks in low whispers to another guard on the other side. That man disappears with an echo of his footsteps. I wait, standing in the middle of the room, until a plain-faced Deacon enters.

"We need to talk about Jack," I say.

The Deacon motions for me to sit. I don't want to, but I also don't want to piss this guy off. I sit.

"I saw Jack. Your terms for repenting are kind of harsh," I say.

"To repent, it's sacrifice, a sacrifice of the soul, of the body. Jesus suffered, died and was buried—"

"Jack's already dead. He's no Jesus. What is the point in causing him harm?"

The Deacon presses his lips together for a moment before answering, "Your kind wouldn't understand."

I stand. "This is ridiculous. Your people made a deal with the Archangels."

"And it's a deal we'd like to deliver. To repent, he must learn to never walk down that sinful path again. Raguel's lesson obviously had no lasting results for you."

"Oh, of all the bullshit."

"Not here, Meg," the Deacon scolds me. "Keep your voice down. The others will hear you."

I can take a lot, but the Deacons beating the sins out of Jack, I can't sit back and watch that. I want Nightingale to wake up and I don't want to go back to that jail in Heaven, but I can't let this continue.

"Let him out," I demand.

"He can leave on his own. But I'll warn you, if he doesn't make it to Heaven, the outlook is not so good for you."

I stand and head for the door. I walk out of the Safe House. As the guard locks the gate behind me, I find Jack and head toward him.

"Hey." I wave to get his attention.

Jack meets me at the fence. "What did you find out?"

I shake my head. "It's not going to get better."

A long moment of silence passes.

"You can leave. You just have to tell them," I say.

"Ca—caw!" Reuben is suddenly standing next to me.

"Holy shit!" I reach out to slap him, but the shackle around my neck tightens until I can't breathe.

Reuben focuses on Jack. "Don't you dare leave that Safe House," he warns. "You have to ascend to Heaven."

"Stop, let her go," Jack begs. "She said we'd find another way."

"There is no other way," Reuben warns, a strange garbling in his throat begins. "You walk the path the Deacons have arranged. That's it."

I drop to the ground, clawing at the metal around my neck.

"Stop," Jack shouts. "I'll stay. Stop hurting her and I'll stay."

The shackle loosens until I can breathe again, but I make no attempt to get up.

Reuben walks away. Probably back to that open field to hunt more worms. The guy has been pecking at the ground nearly nonstop.

"You okay?" Jack asks. He's crouched down and reaching between the criss-cross wires of the fence.

"Fine," I croak.

His hand settles on my shoulder. I focus on the throbbing in his wrist, the blood flowing. I'm so hungry. Those snacks in the trunk have barely touched my aching gut. I could so easily tip my head and bite into—

I roll away from Jack and stumble to my feet. "We'll figure something out. Just give me some time."

Jack nods and backs away, eyeing me warily.

I watch Jack each day as he takes his daily walk around the perimeter of the fence. At least they give him time outside. When I was here, they kept me locked in my cell. I only got to leave when they took me to be questioned relentlessly by those three men behind the desk.

I decide to take a short walk down the road that leads to the Safe House.

There was a time when I would have told all these people to fuck off. I would have done what I wanted to do. When did I get so soft?

"Ca—caw!" Reuben calls.

I stop in my tracks and turn to face him. "What do you want?"

"Where do you think you're going?" he asks.

"I'm taking a walk." I step away from him.

"You didn't ask me."

"Are you my nanny or something?" I kick dirt at him.

The hollow thump of one of the walking dead smacking

into a tree echoes. Reuben is making too much noise, calling them closer.

"Go back to the car," he demands.

"No. I'm just going to take a short walk down this road and clear my head."

Reuben squawk-laughs. "There's not much space in that brain for thinking. Don't forget I spent plenty of time with you on the Earthen plane. I know your kind."

I'd like to kick him in the balls. I wonder if he even has balls anymore?

"Go back. Now," he says.

I push my hands into my pockets and walk in a slow circle. My fingers brush against something, I reach further down, grasp it between my fingers and pull it out. Shit. It's the blue feather from my balcony, been carrying the sucker around in my pocket for a while now.

The hairs on my arms and back of my neck stand, the feeling rushing toward my scalp. The feather sparks and I see...

A wave of darkness. Blood, pooling on the floor, dripping from my mouth. A strength I've never felt before. I'm flying, soaring through the sky then hurtling toward earth like a rocket until everything goes black.

Feeling like I've just run a thousand miles, I groan and roll over.

Reuben is standing over me. There's blood splatter on his shirt.

"What happened to you?" I ask.

"Since no one was available to ward off the dead, I had to take care of them."

It's about time he made himself useful. "So you are capable

of lifting a finger to help." I roll and push off the ground, moving to my feet.

As I'm leaning forward, the shackle falls off my neck and hits the ground with a *clunk*. The metal starts to smolder, melting and smoking until it is nothing more than a puddle of shiny fluid in the dirt.

I glance up.

Reuben's eyes go wide. "No!" he shouts. He's read my record; he knows what I'm going to do next.

I run.

Take Me Home Tonight

I SHOULD HAVE KNOWN something strange would happen. The last time I touched one of my mother's feathers, I couldn't travel between realms for days. But this time, her magic was actually useful. My shoulders have never felt lighter, not having that shackle around my neck. I can finally take deep breaths without feeling like a dog on a leash.

Leaving Reuben in the dust to stare at me with his birdbeak gaping open in shock, I run as fast as I can down the road.

My throat is dry, my muscles weak. I'm free from the grasp of the Deacons and Archangels, but days with no food have taken their toll. My thighs are burning. Adrenaline can only take me so far.

I need help.

"Sparrow!" I yell to the sky. "Sparrow! Help me!"

Moans echo from the forest. My shouting draws the dead. I shouldn't yell and draw such attention in the full daylight, but I can't help myself. I glance over my shoulder to check on Reuben and find him running after me. His gut is filled from days of pecking at the soil. I know that he's going to catch me.

"SPARROW!" I scream. I'm pumping my arms, running fast but feeling like I'm in one of those dreams where you're moving in slow motion.

"Ca—caw!" Reuben calls as he chases me. "You're going straight back to that angel prison, Meg," he threatens.

In this moment, I put all my faith in the lack of treading on his Chuck's. If he had chosen better footwear, he'd probably have caught me by now.

"Jack will become one of Lucifer's minions and that will be on your shoulders," Reuben shouts.

The walking dead are starting to filter out of the forest. I pass the rambling corpses; it's the ones just ahead, trickling out onto the road, that worry me. I doubt I'll be able to outrun Reuben and fight them off.

"Please, Sparrow," I whisper, moving one hand to grasp the hilt of my blade. I envision myself leaping through the air, chopping heads and taking names, and still out running Reuben. It's not going to happen though. There is no room in my chest for defeat and that racing-in-your-ribcage feeling of getting caught. I'm running out of options.

A shadow blocks out the sun.

The moans of the dead multiply.

The shadow moves closer, wings beating fast as a butterfly but dark as Hellnight. Hope blooms in my chest, edging out defeat.

I'm getting closer to the dead.

Reuben is on my heels.

The shadow is so close. I can make out arms and legs. I can usually recognize Sparrow from a mile away but this figure is unfamiliar. Maybe he's grown? It wouldn't be that odd, he's gained mass since he became a Hellion.

My throat burns. I raise my arms to the sky as the shadow swoops in. The figure moves just enough for me to recognize that it is not Sparrow come to save me. It's a Hellion.

Oh, shit.

I scream. I scream so loud that I'm sure every dead soul in a fifteen-mile radius hears me.

Large hands grip me by the arms and lift me into the sky. The Hellion isn't quick enough though. Reuben grabs my ankles. I cry out as he dangles. The Hellion shakes me like a stick. My left shoulder pops out of place. Between screaming in fear and screaming in pain, I kick my feet and scrape the sides of my shoes against Reuben's hands until he gives up and drops to the ground.

The Hellion shifts my weight. He's trying to move his free arm under my legs but I'm kicking and screaming, clawing at his arms and face with my good arm. "Let go of me! Sparrow! Help!"

The Hellion yells back at me in some strange Hellspeak that I don't understand. He's flying over the treetops and alters his body so we're flying up and up and up into the sky.

"Put me down!" I kick him in the stomach. "Don't touch me!"

"Be still!" He yells so loudly that my hair blows away from my face.

"I don't want your hands on me." I have a troubled past with the Hellions. So troubled that I prefer not to be near any of them. Ever.

"Fine with me." The Hellion releases me.

I drop, free-falling thought the sky; the forest of Hell not an inviting cushion.

"Meg!" I recognize Sparrow's voice, the sound of beating wings, and the feeling of his arms as he catches me mid-air.

I choke, never having been so scared in my life. With two feet on the ground I'm determined to do just about anything to save my life. But in the air, I can't fly. I grip Sparrow tight around his neck with my good arm; the other hangs limp at my side. I wrap my legs around his middle and hold on for dear life.

"She doesn't have wings?" I recognize the voice of the Hellion who dropped me.

"No," Sparrow says.

"*Hmrph*," the Hellion grunts. He sounds completely disgusted with the prospect. He isn't the first. "She's injured. Heard her shoulder pop out of joint."

Sparrow shifts his body, tucking my injured arm between us. Then he's flying parallel to the ground. The wind whistles by my ears as we soar, I recognize the path. We're headed to the burning caves.

Sparrow lands at the mouth of the burning caves, the rear entrance of Lucifer's castle. He carries me inside and I let him. Every step he takes jostles my limp arm, causing searing pain in my left shoulder. I've had plenty of injuries in my life, but none have ever hurt this badly. Well, there was that one time that Jim strung me up like a turkey and stabbed me in the chest, but this is a different kind of pain.

"It's okay," Sparrow assures me as he turns at the stairwell and walks down a level. He takes me to the guest room that I stayed in last time I was here.

The giant Hellion follows us the entire time. I glance at him over Sparrow's shoulder. The beast ignores me. He's nearly as big as my father and bald, with horny numbs covering his head.

"The bed or the chair?" Sparrow asks.

The room looks the same as the last time I was here. "The chair, next to the window."

Sparrow sets me down. "Call on Clea," he commands the Hellion.

The songbirds are pecking at seed on the balcony.

Sparrow crouches beside me. "We've been tracking you for days." He shakes his head. "I couldn't get close." He grips his hands into fists. "I've never felt so helpless. Even with all this power."

"It was Reuben, the Deacons, and Archangels." I lean back in the chair. I glance at the door. "That Hellion."

"Skeele?"

"Whatever." I don't care what his name is. "I don't want him near me. Not him, not the others."

"They're not like the groups before," Sparrow says. "They know that they are not to touch you, death is the only punishment for such an offense."

"I don't think they care."

Sparrow's brow rises. He blinks, his irises turning a burning-coal red. "They do. I promise you." He blinks again and the Ireland grass green color returns.

I lean away from him. "What did Lucifer do to you?"

Sparrow shakes his head and stands. He rubs his hand over his face. "It's the darkness."

Clea bursts into the room. "Oh, child!" She rushes to my side. "You're injured."

I motion to my arm.

Her cool fingers touch my skin.

"Can you wave your hands and fix it?" I ask.

"I can heal injuries and illness, but a bone out of place is a bone that needs to be put back into place." She gives me a look, it's a mom look, one that tells me this is going to hurt like a sonofabitch.

She takes my arm, pulls it straight, bends it just right and pops it back to where it belongs.

"Mother of God!" I groan and hold my shoulder.

"Well, now that that's fixed." Clea leans away from me. "When is the last time you were clean?"

There's dried blood on my jeans from Raguel's lashing. My mother healed my back when I first arrived here with Reuben. She left me a clean shirt but that's it. I've been roaming around in the same thing that Reuben dragged me out of the Earthen plane in.

"I could use a shower."

Clea nods in agreement. "After, we'll sling your arm."

I get up and walk to the bathroom, happy to see that the closet here is still full of my clothing.

I close the bathroom door and lock it. Getting undressed is the hardest. My arm moves but it hurts like heck. I wash weeks worth of grime and dried blood off myself. I wash my hair twice, wondering the entire time how Sparrow—or anyone else—could have come within a foot of my stinking hide.

After the shower, I wrap myself in a towel and head for the closet. I've missed the clothing my mother stocked it with. I find a pair of dark wash jeans, a tank, leather jacket, and knee-high boots.

Sparrow shows up as I'm getting dressed. "Do you need help? Clea said you shouldn't be using that arm."

"Ah..." I've got my underwear on and jeans pulled up but unbuttoned. My shoulder does ache. "Sure."

Sparrow's thick fingers begin buttoning my jeans. He zips my fly like a gentleman, then reaches for the tank. I've never had a man dress me before, and when he's bent in front of me, tying and buckling my boots, I almost wish he could dress me every day.

Sparrow stands. He seems so different. When I saw him in Key West at that bar and took him back to my hotel room he was so intense. Now he seems so relaxed and... at home. I think he's beginning to feel comfortable in Hell.

"Just surviving." He smirks as though he's read my mind.

My stomach grumbles.

"You're hungry. I could tell when you were with the Scarecrow." He loosens the collar of his leather vest. Sparrow offers his neck.

The bloodlust is hard to resist and there is no cure, only remission and relapse. It's still something I haven't come to terms with. I'm embarrassed, disgusted with myself. "I can't." I back away from him.

"Meg, this is what we are." He steps closer to me.

"Oh good, you're dressed." Clea enters the room with fabric for a sling.

Sparrow steps away from me, he mutters something about "a job to do" and leaves.

I exhale a breath, completely frustrated with everything. Don't get me wrong, I want Sparrow more than I've ever wanted anything in my life but I must get back to Jack.

"Bend your arm," Clea instructs. Her cold fingers brush my skin as she creates a sling. "How's that?"

The soreness in my shoulder is relieved. "Better." She has the power to heal me fully. "Why don't you fix it?" I ask.

She smiles, it's sly. "Rest, child," Clea offers. "When you wake, we'll discuss your predicament further."

Now that the adrenaline from escaping Reuben has worn off, I do feel exhausted. And I don't feel like arguing with her. I've healed plenty on my own without her intervention. I guess I should just be happy that she put my shoulder back in place.

"I have to get Jack," I say as I'm making my way to the bed. I don't bother taking off my boots. I've grown accustomed to sleeping in shoes and being ready to run.

"Sleep." She touches my forehead and I'm out.

———

I OPEN my eyes to an incessant tapping sound. Sitting up straight, I see where it's coming from. Noah's here and he's tapping his fingers on the table.

"Noah!" I leap from the bed, stopping in my tracks when I notice the look on his face. "What's wrong?"

"I'm here." His tone is flat.

"I take it you're not happy about that."

"If I'm here, Nightingale is in the Astral plane. Alone." He crosses his arms.

Alone and pregnant. I feel for Nightingale, I've been there before. At least she's safe in the Astral. She could definitely be worse places.

"Why are you here?" I ask.

"Your grandfather called me back to be your *manservant* again while you're here."

He says manservant with such disdain. We had so much fun

before. Then shit got fucked up, again. That seems to be a repeating theme in my life.

"What do you want to eat?" Noah snaps.

I blink, emotion clogs my throat. I risked so much for Noah and Nightingale. Maybe Lucifer was right, maybe friendship is petty, right now it seems like it doesn't mean much to Noah.

"Eggs, toast, coffee, and fried chicken."

Noah disappears.

I stand near the table. Songbirds are perched on the railing; chirping, blinking their beady eyes, tilting their heads expectantly. I walk out onto the balcony and find the bin of birdseed. I lay out a thick line of seed. This feels familiar, comforting even, a daily ritual I could so easily go back to.

The clattering of dishes causes me to turn. Noah's back and I get the distinct feeling that I might be eating my breakfast off the floor.

"I didn't ask for this," I say as I step back into the room. "I just need to eat something and then I'll figure out how to get Jack to ascend, get him to Heav—"

"You'll do no such thing." Lucifer is standing in my room, looking intimidating as ever. "That soul is *mine*." He walks toward me. "I own it. Not those assholes in Heaven."

I look up, trying to ignore the weak feeling in my gut.

"If you intervene, things will not bode well for you, granddaughter." He crosses his arms.

What do I do? What do I do? What do I do? I can't leave Jack. I can't leave Nightingale in the Astral.

"As far as the Archangels are concerned, I am a felon. There's a price on my head of 400 souls. I have to bring Jack to Heaven."

"No!" Lucifer shouts.

I will agree that my grandfather is the darkest being I have ever encountered. He shows mercy to no one, except his ghost of a daughter. There was a time that he owed me a favor, I could have saved it for this moment, but I used it on another. I tend to do that: errors in judgment. But, I do know one thing; I spent most of my life being treated like crap. I'm not standing for it any longer.

"This is none of your concern." I straighten my back and tip my chin up.

"Like Hell it isn't," he bellows.

I glance at Noah, who looks mortified.

"I have to get Jack to Heaven. It's the only way they'll release me for killing Remiel."

Lucifer's face goes slack for a moment. Then he breaks into loud laughter. "You killed *him*? Of all the Archangels."

"Unfortunately." I carry a lot of guilt over the incident.

Lucifer laughs and shakes his head in disbelief. "He was a dick."

"Well, he's dead. And Nightingale is pregnant and won't wake up. She won't leave the Astral plane. She's been hiding there with Noah." I try to explain the predicament I'm in.

Lucifer glances at my manservant. He doesn't seem impressed. "Oh yes, lost souls and revelry. Not on my turf. My house. My rules. You'll go nowhere."

The door to my room slams closed.

The lock engages.

Lucifer disappears in a cloud of smoke.

"No!" I run to the door and bang on it. I try to the handle but the thing might as well be made of solid stone.

"You took him from me!" Nightingale is in my dreams once again. She's so pale, her belly distended in the late month of pregnancy. *"Send him back. I want him back!"* she's screaming at me.

"Night..." I open my mouth to try and explain, but there is nothing except pain in my jaw as all my teeth wobble and fall out of my head. There's blood pouring out of my mouth, dripping at my feet.

"You'll send him back to me, now!"

My eyes snap open.

Noah is sitting in a chair next to the window, brooding. All he needs is a few piercings and a flannel shirt wrapped around his waist.

"Did you see her in your dreams?" he asks.

"Nightingale?" I should know better than to ask, there's only one her to him.

"Yeah." I sit up and move off the bed.

"And?"

"She wants you back."

I head to the closet and get dressed. What does one wear on escape day? I choose a pair of dark jeans, layer a tank with a long-sleeved top, then a leather jacket. As I'm dressing, I recall the tips Jim gave me so long ago before this mess, when he was training me to survive the apocalypse. Dress in layers, always wear stable boots, carry a dry pair of socks and keep your bug out bag nearby. I bend and pull on a pair of boots. Then I head to the bathroom to brush my teeth.

"Where are you going?" Noah asks.

"On an *adventure*."

Now he looks interested.

"I can't get you back to Nightingale until I make it back to that Safe House."

I cross the room, open the balcony door, step out and glance over the balcony. We are more than a few flights up, but the stone juts out just enough that I might be able to climb down.

I throw my leg over the railing.

"What are you doing?" Noah asks.

"Getting out of here. I'll be damned if he thinks he can lock me up."

"What happened to you just *poofing* everywhere?"

I point to my arm. "Injuries inhibit that." I pull my arm out of the sling and begin climbing down.

Noah follows.

There's a horde of the dead below us, jaws chomping, moaning like tipped cows, stinking up my air with their rotting aroma. I cough, trying not to gag.

"So what's the plan once you get down?" Noah asks.

"I have to get back to Auburn. Jack's there."

"About that..." Noah looks suddenly sad.

"Yeah?"

"I can't believe he's dead."

What do you say to one of your best friends who just found out their brother died? I say the only think I can think of, "Only the good die young, my friend."

"You think the people back in Gouverneur miss us?"

"They probably miss Jack."

"Probably," he agrees.

"Just think, all this life after death. There's so much more that we didn't know about, that all those people back in Gouverneur don't know about. You and Jack died, but you're still living."

"What happens when you die?" Noah asks.

"Clea said, I'll go where my soul belongs."

"Where's that?"

I shake my head. "I have no idea."

"Going somewhere?" I recognize the voice of Skeele behind me.

I turn to find him hovering in the air, wings beating slowly to keep him elevated.

"Go away," I tell him.

"I can't do that." He moves closer.

I edge away. "Don't touch me."

"Don't touch her, man," Noah warns.

Skeele crosses his arms. "You're in deep shit."

"Usually," I reply. It's a repeating theme in my life and no longer surprises me.

"You're not going to like yourself one bit when you find out how much this little escape is going to cost you."

"There's nothing little about this escape." I move down another few feet. "I'm climbing down the face of Lucifer's castle. This is the worst escape ever."

Skeele mutters something in Hellspeak.

"Can you leave now?" I ask. "I have shit to do."

"Sparrow sent me." He crosses his arms. "I will not leave you. That is my order."

"He really shouldn't have." I told Sparrow I didn't want any of the Hellions near me.

"Would you like help down?" Skeele asks.

"I'd rather plummet to my death." I keep descending.

"Your funeral," he says as he flies away.

I stop for a moment to rest my sweating face against the

cool stone of the castle. My arms feel like rubber and my thighs are burning.

"He's just standing down there," Noah says.

I turn and notice Skeele's figure on the ground. He stands at the edge of the forest. Waiting.

I keep climbing.

"Your inability to poof is a real inconvenience," Noah complains.

"Shut up."

I stop a few feet above the heads of the horde of the dead. They're reaching for us, clawing at the stone of Lucifer's castle hoping to get a bite.

"What's your plan?" Noah asks.

There are a few things I could do: wait until sunset when they're sleeping, try to inch my way to the edge of the horde and hope they don't follow, or jump in the middle of them with my blade blazing and run for it. I've never had a problem outrunning the dead, my aching shoulder shouldn't make a difference now.

Sweat is dripping into my eyes. So much for that shower. Seems these days I can't keep clean for more than an hour.

As I'm trying to decide what to do, Skeele walks closer. The dead part for him, leaving a clear path for us. I jump down. Noah follows. The dead hiss and chomp their dangling jaws as we pass.

"Neat trick," I tell Skeele.

He keeps walking. "I suppose you're going back to the Safe House in Auburn."

"Yes."

"Follow me." He walks along the edge of the forest, finally

leading us under the canopy when he arrives at a well-beaten path.

"Where's Sparrow?" I finally ask.

"Making a deal with the devil," Skeele replies.

"Why?"

"You think Lucifer was just going to let you waltz out of there against his wishes? Clea and Sparrow just went to war with him to allow you to go free and continue on your *mission*. Rules that you have no inkling of have been broken and Lucifer will have redemption."

We exit the forest. A dark blue Jeep Wrangler is parked on the side of the road. Skeele opens the passenger side door and motions for me and Noah to get in.

I pause. "This is convenient."

"Sparrow knew you'd escape. He planned this."

"Of course he did." I crawl in the Jeep and Noah follows.

Skeele gets behind the wheel and starts driving. He takes Highway 220, driving faster than I would ever trust myself to drive on the north country roads of NY, and I know those roads well.

Sparrow

Lucifer was deep in thought as Sparrow and Clea stood before him. Sparrow glanced up at the hissing sound coming from the shadows on the ceiling above.

"Your proposition is barely sufficient," Lucifer said as he set the contract down on the desk. "This is the greatest sinner we are talking about. A murderer. A killer. That soul is *mine*." Lucifer slammed his giant hands down on the desk and stood. His large wings snapped open, extending nearly the width of the giant room.

"Daddy," Clea started. "If you'd just—"

"Silence!" Lucifer was staring Sparrow down. "You have worked at my side long enough to know that this is not an acceptable offer."

Sparrow bowed, feeling the darkness and light warring within him. He knew what Meg would want, what she would hate, what would make her hate him, possibly. "Sir, she's your granddaughter."

Lucifer laughed.

Sparrow remembered a time when Lucifer would bend to the will of his daughter and granddaughter; he'd protected both of them when necessary. Sparrow couldn't understand why now was so different. Well, he had a feeling he knew what Lucifer wanted and why he was being so difficult, but Sparrow wasn't going to give up so easily.

"Yes, the granddaughter who was given the greatest wish, and she used it on your sister. She could have saved *you*, but she didn't. And yet, you stand before me risking everything for her." Lucifer sat again. He snapped his fingers and the contract Sparrow had brought went up in flames, the parchment turning black, ash fluttering away on the draft in the room.

Clea cast an uneasy glance at Sparrow.

"Is there a counter-offer?" Sparrow asked.

Lucifer laughed again. "I'm not here to counter you, son. I'm waiting for you to give me an offer I can't refuse."

Clea attempted to reason with him once more. "Daddy—"

"Silence!" There was fire in Lucifer's eyes when he looked at his daughter. She was simply a soul in its final resting place, but a soul with magical powers, nonetheless. Whatever magic she had over Lucifer was not working this time.

Sparrow had had enough conversations with Clea to know that Lucifer would never forgive her for running off, pregnant with Gabriel's child. Meg was the half breed of that liaison. And Meg had the ouroboros, something that no one except for Lucifer seemed to know the meaning of, not that Sparrow hadn't searched endlessly for the meaning of that mark on her upper thigh. So far, all they knew was the birthmark was one of the reasons why she could flutter between realms, that and her soul not knowing where it belonged.

Lucifer made a dark grumbling sound deep in his throat.

Sparrow knew that this meant he was losing patience.

"Double my term," Sparrow offered.

Lucifer smiled, it was sinister, his lips spreading thin, revealing sharp teeth. His giant wings shuttered with anticipation.

Damn, this was exactly what he wanted.

"You can't," Clea whispered.

"One more peep from you, daughter, and I'll punish you like I should have that day you told me Gabriel knocked you up," Lucifer threatened.

"But—you can't—you can't do this!" Clea was raising her voice and the creatures in the shadows slithered faster and faster the louder she became. "You can't let him stay down here any longer than necessary. You know it will upset the balance. It will—"

Lucifer snapped his fingers and Clea disappeared into thick air. The King of Hell cleared his throat and waved his hand, palm up, in expectation. "Insubordinate little shit that one is. Love her to death but little girls just wrap you right around their fingers. She hasn't been punished in a few hundred years, this is long overdue." Lucifer chuckled. "This will be good to remember if you're ever gifted a daughter. Now, you were saying, son." Lucifer's brows rose in greedy anticipation.

Sparrow's guts twisted. "Let Jack Cooper ascend to Heaven, let Meg go, and double my term as a Hellion."

"Hm." Lucifer tapped his fingers together under his chin. "That soul is worth plenty. The last I heard from the Deacons they were acquiring four hundred souls for him. I'm not so sure a double—"

"Two and a half terms." Meg was going to kill him, Sparrow knew with every spec of his being. She'd tear him limb from limb.

"Now we're getting somewhere." Lucifer stood and paced the room, shadows quivering as he neared then extending their reach as he passed in a twisted ebb and flow. "Just to make it clear, now you're asking for two favors." Lucifer held two fingers in the air. "Two favors but *just* two and a half terms. Now, I've been the King of Hell for eons, and I might have forgotten some of my math, but I know four hundred plus one out of control half breed does not equal two point five terms."

"Triple my term," Sparrow offered.

Lucifer slammed his hands down on the desk, his smile spread wide. "Now we're talking, son! Come on. *Come on!* Make me an offer I can't refuse, you're bargaining with Satan. Make your father proud!"

"Four terms." Sparrow's mouth had gone dry. The darkness was rising within him, tendrils of gray wrapping around his soul and threatening to drag it under for good.

"Sold!" Lucifer snapped his fingers and spun on one foot.

A new parchment appeared on his desk. Lucifer lifted a pen

and handed it to Sparrow. "Oh, the things you've done for my granddaughter. Meg should be proud." Lucifer clapped his hands loudly with excitement. "This is getting *dangerous!* Destiny will have my balls in a vice."

Sparrow bent to sign the contract before it rolled up and flew across the room, settling into a pigeonhole in the wall where thousands of contracts such as his were stored.

"I've always loved a good challenge. How about you?"

"There was a time that I did." Sparrow remembered his time as Legion Commander for Gabriel's Kingdom, he also remembered a man that he'd never be again.

Meg

We're barely to the busted sign for the New York border, when something drops from the sky and stands in the road before us.

Skeele slams on the breaks.

The Jeep comes to a halt.

Sparrow is standing in the middle of the road. His wings waver for a moment before he tucks them tight against his back. He doesn't look happy but that doesn't stop him from walking toward the Jeep. He walks like he's on a mission, like there's one thing on his mind.

"Uh oh," Skeele mutters. "Everyone out. He doesn't look happy."

I get out of the Jeep as Sparrow moves closer. He stops to talk quietly with Skeele for a moment. "Wait for us," he orders Skeele before heading in my direction.

"Sparrow?" I ask.

"Meg. You're not in your room."

"I have to get Jack."

With a smirk he says, "Of course you do. Always a savior for your friends."

Ouch. That hurts. In all the time I've known Sparrow, it's the first time he's ever pointed it out. I'm not sure if he knows I'd do anything for him as well.

Sparrow wraps his arms around me, bends his knees and lifts off into the sky.

"What are you doing?" I ask before we're over the treetops.

"I need you, Meg. And you need me." He licks my neck. "Stop denying it."

I'll take a trip to pound-town whenever he wants, but he seems angry right now. It makes me nervous. "Where are we going?"

"Some place private."

We are in the air only for a few minutes. Sparrow descends, landing in an open field. He pushes my jacket off my shoulders.

I lick my lips. "Out in the open like this?"

"No better place right now. The dead are sleeping for the night." He grips the hem of my shirt and pulls it over my head. Next he begins working on the button of my jeans. "Say yes. Please, Meg. Say yes."

How could I ever deny him? "Yes."

I kick my boots off. Sparrow shucks my jeans down my legs. I begin working on the leather ties of his vest. He's working on the ties of his pants.

He stands naked before me in the sepia moonlight, looking less like an unsure Hellion who has lost his memories and more like a Deity who knows exactly what he wants.

Sparrow drops to his knees. "We will be invincible together." He presses his lips to my abdomen. His hands slide up my back, unhook my bra and toss it away. Sliding down, his fingers hook the elastic of my underwear and he pulls them off.

Me and Sparrow, naked in a field in Hell about to do the dirty in the moonlight, I'd never guessed it.

He's looking at my tattoos. His fingers brush over the watercolor of the sparrow in flight on my chest.

"You are mine and I am yours," he reminds me.

"Yes." We are always repeating these terms to each other, never seeming to come to fruition. I wonder when we'll stop fluttering around the edges of what we are and what we will become, when will we dive deep into the abyss of what is to come?

Sparrow's mouth is on me. I push my fingers into his hair and hold on for dear life. His hands grip my ass and press me harder to his face. A few moments later he's pulling me down to the grass with him. He takes my hand, kisses the back of it before nipping and licking his way up my arm to my shoulder. He bites the tender skin there, sucks. I moan his name and wrap my legs around his narrow waist. He licks my shoulder and moves to my neck, his tongue pressing over the pulse of my jugular.

"This." He sounds out of breath. "I can't get enough of this."

Just as he fills me, his teeth pierce my skin. I open my eyes; Sparrow's own pulse calls me. He kisses me, his tongue in my mouth. I taste my own blood. "Don't be afraid." He presses into me again, filling me in one strong thrust.

I can't deny it any longer. I give in, press my lips to his neck, lick his salty skin, and sink my teeth in.

Oh, the taste of his blood, dark and sweet and the tang of danger.

———

Sparrow's collecting my clothes from where we dropped them in the field. We dress in silence. My mind is churning. The self-loathing of drinking blood burns. Sparrow senses this.

"Stop." His hands are on my face, his eyes looking into mine. "Embrace it. We can never go back to what we were. We can never go back."

"You'll never go back to Heaven?"

"That's not what I said."

I pull my jacket on. He may not have said those words exactly, but I get the sense that he'll never be an Angel again. He had to do his time as a Hellion so darkness would taint his soul. He had to know darkness to rule, but something has gone wrong along the way. My grandfather doesn't seem to want to release Sparrow from his term as a Hellion.

"What are these?" Sparrow is holding my arms up, inspecting the rune tattoos.

"They're supposed to hide me from ethereal beings."

Sparrow traces his fingers across the black ink. "Hide you?" He tips his head. "I can see you just fine."

"That's because you know who I am. Jed said—"

"Who is Jed?" Sparrow blinks and his eyes flash with burnished orange flames of suspicion.

I step back. "A tattoo artist." I point to the watercolor of the sparrow in flight on my chest. "The guy who did this. You've met him."

"You let him touch you, again?"

I'm having a hard time deciding if Sparrow is currently jealous or concerned.

"I had to do something. The Deacons were chasing me down." I walk away from Sparrow and find my jacket.

"They were chasing you?" He shakes his head. "If you'd just stay with me. You'd be safer." He stalks toward me.

"Maybe you should stay with me," I counter.

"The curse—"

"Yeah. Yeah." I know he must cure his family of the crazy Angel curse. I don't mind him being crazy—I'm selfish, always have been. If it weren't for Nightingale, I'd tell him to embrace the curse.

At the edge of the field, I notice a shadow which looks suspiciously like the figure of a man with a giant birdhead. Reuben is there, watching. I wonder how much he saw? I'm not shy but I'm not an exhibitionist, the thought of Reuben watching us chills me.

"He can't enter the field," Sparrow says.

"Why's that?"

He points to a stone archway nearby that I didn't notice. "Hallowed ground. He must be accompanied by higher being to enter and cross the threshold."

"He's going to follow us," I warn.

"Expect him to." Sparrow doesn't seem intimidated at all. In fact, he sets off across the field, walking directly toward Reuben.

"She has a task to finish," Reuben says as he points at me.

Sparrow slaps Reuben's hand away. "She'll finish your task. But you don't touch her. You don't come within five feet of her unless I say so."

Wow, I've never seen him so possessive before. But then, I guess he's got a right to the feeling. He had to stand by and watch all this time I've been with Reuben, never able to intervene. I'd say with Sparrow's history, that has got to be the worst.

We walk our way to the Jeep, Reuben following. I get the feeling that Sparrow thinks Reuben's crow head is a little too awesome. Unique bird attributes always sway the guy.

"Oh no," Noah exclaims when he gets a good look at Reuben. "Hell no. I am not riding with that thing."

"Me either." I glance at Reuben. He's lucky I don't kill him on the spot. The only reason I haven't is because I fear going back to that prison in Heaven and I need to use him to communicate with the Deacons.

"He can ride on the back bumper," Skeele says.

That's the best suggestion I've ever heard. We're on the same page. I might actually like Skeele.

"You drive," Sparrow points at Skeele.

"Flying is faster," Skeele offers.

Sparrow glances at me.

"Oh, forgot about little miss no wings." The edge of Skeele's lip tips up, as though he were about to smile. I don't think I want him to smile. With those horns covering his head, I can only imagine what his teeth look like.

"Let us in," I tell the Safe House guard. His keys jingle as he unlocks the gate. "You two cannot enter." He points at Sparrow and Skeele.

Sparrow whispers something to Skeele and Skeele turns and takes off into the sky.

"I will enter," Sparrow tells the guard. He blinks, no doubt showing the guard the fire in his eyes.

The guard pulls the gate wide open but keeps his distance from us. "You know the risk."

We walk the path to the door and head inside.

The men from the desk-of-questioning are waiting in the Qualifiers room. Usually you don't see these guys until Quarantine, when they question you relentlessly. I'm not sure what their power is, but to see them out here, defending the Safe House against us, it must be significant.

One of them points at Sparrow, his robe flowing. "Your kind is forbidden in here."

"Bring out Jack and I'll leave." Sparrow crosses his arms, waiting.

We wait for nearly an hour. The air is tense, mostly because I'm filled with nervous energy. I don't want to go back to that cell in Heaven, but I can't sit back and watch Jack deteriorate.

Finally, footsteps echo. Jack is on the other side of the door, dressed in his regular clothes again. I worry about how gaunt he looks and what the Deacons did to him during the few days that I was away.

"Jack?" I move toward him. "Are you okay?"

The guard opens the door and shoves him through. "Good luck, sinner," the guard mutters.

"Noah?" Jack whispers.

The brothers embrace. It's heartwarming, well, besides the fact that they're both dead and in Hell.

"Let's get out of here," Sparrow says.

Reuben hasn't said a word. Makes me wonder what's going on behind his beady eyes.

"But, I didn't repent. I didn't do what they told me." Jack looks worried.

"Just keep walking." I take Jack's elbow and urge him out of the Safe House. "We'll figure something out."

A feeling comes over me as we're walking Jack out of the Safe House, it's like we're rescuing him and I feel... proud. I can walk him out of here with a smile, can't say that for anyone who ever picked me up from juvie when I was a kid.

The guard at the gate can't get it locked fast enough after we've passed by.

"I'm sorry, Meg," Jack whispers. "I didn't repent. I don't know if I could have. I know you think I belong in Heaven, but after all that," he motions to the Safe House, "I think I belong in Hell."

"Don't worry about it," I say. "We'll find another way."

We walk to the cruiser that's still parked in the empty Safe House parking lot.

"Let's get this show on the road," Sparrow suggests as he glances at the car. "You need anything from in there before we go?"

"You're coming?" I ask Sparrow, surprised.

"I need to speak with the Council. And I'd like to see my sister." He takes my hand. "Let's do this. Meg," Sparrow motions for me to do something. I just don't know what.

I shake my head. I don't understand.

"You are the one who can travel between realms," he reminds me.

"But I've never been to the Astral plane. I don't even know how to get there."

"You can focus on Nightingale, right? You did something

similar to find your mother's bag of bones and return them here."

Oh yes, it took a lot of energy to find her, but I did simply focus. And I've seen the Astral plane in my dreams. I nod, taking Jack's hand, Noah's hand, and Sparrow's hand. Reuben is watching.

"What about him?" I ask.

"The Deacons will take care of him," Sparrow assures me.

I wink at Reuben and hold in the urge to shout at him that he's an asshole.

I close my eyes and focus.

Poof!

———

THE ASTRAL PLANE is an ever-changing landscape, the place of spirits and dreams. It's different for everyone who enters. For some reason, Noah and Nightingale have settled on a vast, space-like panorama.

"Where is she?" I ask, my voice echoing.

Sparrow grips my hand tighter.

"Night?" Noah asks.

She appears, eyes rimmed in red, belly jutting out and full of child. This is her soul; her body rests in Heaven, awaiting her return. "I thought you'd never return," she says. Nightingale looks up and sees Sparrow. "Brother!" She whistles a light trill as she runs and leaps into his arms.

Sparrow grips her tight. "Night." He buries his face in her shoulder and takes a deep breath. "I've missed you."

"You've finally got your brains back?" she asks with a smile.

"I don't know how I could ever forget you." He whistles a light birdcall. Nightingale whistles a trill back.

It's all very lovely, watching these two communicate with birdcalls.

"Well," Nightingale turns to look at all of us, "you can't all stay here."

"Night," Sparrow grips her shoulder, "you can't stay here, either. You must go home. Now." He touches his open palm to her belly. "This baby. You can't deliver with your soul here and your body back in Heaven. To deliver a soul separate from a body, and on separate planes," he shakes his head, "terrible things will become of the child."

Nightingale's eyes widen. Noah moves to her side and they embrace.

"It's time, Nightingale," Sparrow says.

"But..." Her chin quivers. "I don't want to. I want to stay with Noah. I can't go back there. With you and father both gone they'll force me to marry. I can't. I can't do it."

"Night," Noah starts.

"You go, Noah," Jack interrupts them. "You love her. I'll take your place here." Jack glances around at the vast nothingness.

There is silence after Jack offers to take Noah's place in the Astral and Hell. It's not as simple as a soul for a soul in this equation. Jack committed murder, his soul is worth hundreds, it's worth the price on my head. I glance at Sparrow; it's worth my freedom. I'd let them make the switch in a heartbeat, but my freedom also impacts Sparrow's life. This is no easy decision.

Noah is shaking his head. "It's too late for me. Lucifer already owns me." He turns to Nightingale. "I'll always be there. Always and forever. You and me." He settles a hand on her bulging abdomen. "But you can't stay here. You must face them. We both know this."

"They'll force me to marry," Nightingale warns again.

"I know." Noah never looks away from her.

Jack steps forward. "I'll take care of her." He faces Nightingale. "You don't know me, but I'll take care of you. For Noah, I'll do this."

Nightingale nods in understanding, tears streaming down her face.

"I'll see you in Hell," Noah says to me. "I know it won't be long before you screw things up again."

Noah is tethered to me by Lucifer himself. He can't go to Heaven, but I will see him again, soon, be it the Earthen plane or Hell. I take no offense to his dig, it's true, I always manage to fuck things up.

We take hands, Noah looking on from a distance.

Poof.

We arrive in Sparrow and Nightingale's castle.

Nightingale gasps as she wakes and sits up in the bed.

"Oh no." She grips her belly and lets out a moan. "I think the baby is coming!"

———

NIGHTINGALE SHOVES the pillows behind her back and puffs her cheeks out. I notice her once black wings are now snowy white again. Lucifer tried to hide her with the change when I brought her to Hell.

"What happened to your wings?" I ask.

She moans, her face red. "They molted. Worst experience

ever. *Mmmmh.*" She grips her belly. "Besides this. This definitely ranks up there with molting."

Sparrow is the first one to move. "You better cross your legs and hold that kid in there. You can't deliver until you're married or the Council will burn your hide," Sparrow warns.

Jack is standing in the middle of the room, shading his eyes with his hand and taking it all in. He moves to the window and looks to the landscape below. "This is Heaven?" he whispers.

Nightingale moans and starts puffing her breaths.

"Oh Jesus, what do we do?" I ask. "What do we do?"

"First of all, you do not call *Him* to this delivery!" Nightingale warns.

Sparrow runs out of the room, nothing but a dark shadow that looks completely out of place.

"Meg!" Nightingale is holding her hand out. I take it. She squeezes so hard I feel the bones of my fingers crunching together.

"What do I do?" Jack asks.

"You put this on." Sparrow has reentered the room and throws clothing at Jack. "I'll be damned if my baby sister is going to marry you looking like that."

Jack shakes out the clothes. It's a tux.

Nightingale screams and bends her knees up. "I think he's coming!"

"Oh my G—" She squeezes my fingers and glares. "Easter bunny," I fill in the blank instead of calling the Lord to this birth.

"Go fetch your father, Meg. And Teari too," Sparrow orders.

I focus on my father's kingdom and where he might be.

Poof.

"Of all the bullshit!" Gabriel shouts as I appear out of thin air. "Meg!"

"I need you now." I grab his hand. "Where's Teari?"

"She's at the barrack—"

Poof.

I bring Gabriel along with me to collect her at the barracks. Teari is standing on the sidelines, watching the Legion practice battle.

"Meg?" she asks.

"No time to explain." I grab her hand.

Poof.

We return to the bedroom where Nightingale is about to give birth. Jack's jaw drops open as he looks up at my father.

"She's about to deliver," Sparrow warns Teari.

"Mother of Pearl, Sparrow!" Gabriel crosses the room to greet him. He takes in Sparrow's new look, the leather wings, darkened features and Hellion getup. "Dark looks good on you, boy!" Gabriel flicks him in the forehead. "Bet there's still a bit of glitter hiding in there though."

Sparrow smiles. "Possibly." He glances at Jack who's now dressed in the tux. "More pressing, I need you to wed my sister to him." Sparrow points at Jack. "Before this baby is born and the Council intervenes."

"Well," Gabriel puffs out his chest as he judges Jack. "He's neither Angel nor Demon. What is this?"

"That is the Deacon's 400 soul paycheck," I tell Gabriel. "And my ticket to freedom."

"Ah." Gabriel rubs his chin and seems indecisive. "Wouldn't you rather marry Meg here and run your kingdom?" he asks Sparrow.

"I won't be returning to this kingdom for a while," Sparrow replies.

My blood goes cold.

Before I get a chance to drill him on what exactly *a while means*, Sparrow starts searching the drawers in the room. "They must be wed before the baby is born. I just have to find the rings." He moves on to another dresser, pulling out boxes and clothing. "Ah! Found them." He returns to Gabriel's side with a set of golden rings in his hand. "The royal wedding bands."

Teari is at Nightingale's side, repositioning her, instructing her to breathe slower, in through her nose and out her mouth. I stand near the window, feeling as though I'm looking through a tunnel at the scene before me.

"Well, lets get on with it," Gabriel motions for Jack to move closer. "The Council is going to have a blasted field day with this." He laughs. "I can't wait to rub it in that prick Raguel's face. This is one of the best days of my life!"

Jack is standing at the side of the bed, Nightingale's outstretched hand in his. Gabriel's large hand is covering both of theirs as he speaks in Latin. Sparrow and I watch from the opposite side of the bed, both of us taking in the scene of the wedding and the birth.

Gabriel's talking so fast I can't make out what he's saying.

"Push!" Teari tells Nightingale.

Nightingale's face is bright red; she's nodding to Gabriel as she's pushing the baby out.

Jack looks pale. He did just travel across the ethereal realms and now he's getting married and having a baby, any other guy would probably be crapping their pants right about now.

Jack puts a ring on Nightingale's finger.

Nightingale stops pushing, she's holding her breath,

focusing on getting the ring on Jack's finger. Lining it up just right in a moment of calm, she manages to get it on.

"Now! Push now!" Teari tells Nightingale.

Gabriel is praying at lightning speed, trying to complete this ceremony in record time. Now, I'm holding my breath.

"Hold her leg, Meg!" Teari shouts at me. "Help hold her leg up!"

Gabriel claps his hands and the room goes bright for an instant.

"You're wed!" Gabriel exclaims. "Best wedding ever. I'm going to tell that bastard Raguel." And he walks out of the room.

"Get her other leg!" Teari yells at Jack.

He moves; some color has come back to his face.

I make the mistake of looking down; there are scars on her thighs and dark hair from the baby's head. I close my eyes. I've never prayed for a moment in my life, but remembering what happened to Nightingale—what would have never happened if I had left her here and not brought her to Hell—I know that this baby is either going to be Noah's or part Hellion. I can't bring myself to watch and find out.

Nightingale makes a high-pitched sound. Noises of wetness and Teari muttering to herself fill the room. Someone pushes me away from Nightingale. I keep my eyes pinched closed.

The baby cries.

Nightingale weeps and coos.

"Open your eyes, Meg," Sparrow whispers in my ear.

"I'm too afraid," I whisper back.

"Of what?"

"You know." I can't say it out loud but he must know that

I'm afraid of looking at that baby and finding it with red skin and a head full of horns.

"Your life can't go on until you open your eyes." Sparrow kisses me.

"Are you my monster?"

"I am your monster, your saving grace, your everything." He kisses me again, this time, his lips linger on mine. "And you are mine."

I open my eyes.

Sparrow's smiling. If he's smiling that can only mean that a Hellbaby wasn't just born.

I turn to Nightingale. The baby boy looks like a perfect mixture of her and Noah, porcelain skin, dark eyes and blonde hair.

I smile with relief.

We Didn't Start the Fire

"That is some fucked up, North Country shit, Jack. Normal people don't marry their brother's pregnant girlfriend."

"She's not pregnant anymore." Jack smirks. "So, I'm a king now. You should respect my authority."

"All hail King Jack." I bow, mocking him and laugh. "You've got no authority. She might though." I tip my head toward the bedroom where Nightingale is resting.

He exhales. "I never saw this coming."

"None of us did."

"Meg, I have no idea what I'm doing. I know nothing about this place."

I explain to him what I know of the Seven Kingdoms of Heaven, following it up with, "Nightingale will teach you more. Give her time."

Jack looks away for a moment. "The things I did when I was alive..."

"You're still alive here. This is a continuation of your life."

He rubs his hands through his hair and exhales. "She was with Noah. I am not really a replacement for him."

How could he not know that every chick in town was pining over him? "Jack Cooper, you were voted most eligible bachelor for three years in high school."

"I thought that was only senior year."

"Chicks dig you, Jack." I lean back and look into the bedroom where Nightingale rests with the baby. "She was in love with Noah—still in love with him. Give her some time. Even if she never loves you, you can be friends. That's all a relationship ever really needs."

Jack narrows his eyes. "So you and this Sparrow guy…"

"What about him?"

"Are you friends?"

"It's a bit more complicated than that, but, yes, we started out as friends. He saved my life and I saved his."

I'm wondering where Sparrow is right now. He said that he had to go visit Gabriel, but I haven't seen him in hours.

"So he's like, a demon or something?" Jack asks.

I explain to him the details of Sparrow. How he is Nightingale's brother and is doing his time as a Hellion to break his family's curse. When I mention Nightingale being crazy, Jack interrupts me.

"Wait. I just married some headcase?" he asks.

"She seems to have improved since the last time I saw her." I leave out the details of her communicating with birdcalls and roller-skating everywhere. Of course, he'll probably appreciate the tiny shorts she tends to wear.

Jack rubs his mouth. "I'm just not sure I'm ready to handle all of this." He shakes his head.

"You'll handle it. You figure out how to handle this, Jack, or you go back to Hell and release your soul to the Devil."

Jack's eyes go wide.

"Meg?" Nightingale calls from the bedroom.

I walk away from Jack, leaving him on the balcony to sort things out in his head.

"Hey, Night." The baby is sleeping in her arms.

"You were worried, weren't you?" she asks.

Well, that's a loaded question. I was worried about plenty, but since I don't want to admit to any of it, I'll let her steer the conversation.

Nightingale whistles the eerie tremolo of the loon.

My eyes snap to hers.

"You were worried that this baby was part Hellion," she says.

I nod.

"We have this connection now, Meg." She reaches out to touch my hand. Weeks ago I would have pulled away from her, but right now, I let her touch me. It's the least I can do for all she's been through. "Sparrow says the Hellions will never be like that again. He's done things differently down there, now that he's in charge."

I swallow hard. She's so trusting. With those scars on her thighs, and the scars on my soul, I'm not sure how she could be. I'm not. Maybe it's that angelic part of her, clearly Gabriel's traits never stuck on me.

"Sparrow's different," I change the subject. "Isn't he?"

Nightingale nods. She taps the side of her head. "It seems whatever was scrambled is starting to go right again." The baby in her arms grunts and stretches. "This might be the end of the curse." She runs her fingers over the baby's fine, light hair. "He did it, you know, Meg; he fixed it so I don't have to worry about this child falling down the same rabbit hole as us. No more scrambled brains."

"Night," I ask, "Sparrow mentioned something about birthing the baby with its soul separate from its body, what happens to the baby in that situation?"

She shakes her head. "You don't want to know the answer to that question, Meg." Nightingale adjusts the baby so she's holding him out to me. "Do you want to hold him?"

I still, unable to move. Memories flash through my mind, memories of a pastel decorated nursery, tiny clothes with itty bitty buttons and snaps, white diapers, and a brand-new crib for a baby that never delivered.

I back away.

Nightingale frowns and pulls the baby back to her chest.

"I can't," I say as I turn.

"Meg?" she starts to ask but I leave the room.

I run down the stairs, out the front door, and down the walkway to the garden.

Now that Nightingale is awake, the house staff have returned and I startle a gardener who's planting bushes. He stands, gives me a weary look, and walks away.

My hands shake. I can't touch that baby. I could never touch something so pure and innocent as a baby born into the realm of Heaven. That child will live a life I couldn't; my mother took that from me. She thought she was doing good, birthing me on the Earthen plane, giving me the option to go where I wanted. But in reality, it just messed me up more. I feel like I don't belong anywhere. Not in Heaven, not in Hell, definitely not the Astral. The Earthen plane, though, that is a place where I had begun to feel at home. I spent my life there, got comfortable, and even though I don't belong mingling amongst the pure humans, it's the closest thing to home that I have right now.

Sparrow's walking toward me. His footsteps echo on the stone path, his hands are behind his back.

"What's wrong?" I ask.

"You're going to hate me for this. But know that I am truly sorry. It must be done."

"Wha—" Before I get the words out, he clasps a metal shackle around my neck.

"You asshole!" I reach for my blade but Sparrow rips the holster—blade and all—off my thigh. "What are you doing?"

"I said I was sorry." He backs away from me. "But, I have always wanted to touch your blade. You just never let me."

"I am going to cut off your—"

"For the love of Pete!" Gabriel's voice booms. "Are you ready yet? Let's get this show on the road!"

"One second," Sparrow shouts back.

I still. "What the hell is this all about?"

Sparrow's gaze is darker than black, even in the bright sunlight of Heaven. "I can't tell you now. I just had to make sure you didn't run."

"What makes you think I'd run?"

"Meg, I remember all the times you've run on me. You ran when we caught the snowy owl, you ran when I couldn't remember, you always run. And now, it's time to face the Council." He touches the metal around my neck. "I could have attached a chain to this and then you'd be at my mercy." He smiles before pressing a quick kiss to my lips. Then he bends and lifts me over his shoulder.

"Let me down!" I kick my feet and pound on his sides.

"Unpossible."

"You can't make up words." I press my elbows into his back. "Unpossible isn't even a real word."

Sparrow laughs. "I can do what I want." He slaps my ass.

I STAND BEFORE THE COUNCIL, heavy metal around my neck, on the brink of exhaustion after traveling through realms and the excitement of a wedding and a birth. I was hoping to never see this place again. My back still aches at remembering the time alone with Raguel. He's more wicked than I could ever dream of being.

Raguel is giving me the stink-eye, when he's not glaring at Sparrow's leathery wings. "And how is it that a being such as yourself crossed into this realm?" he asks Sparrow.

"Magic." Sparrow's voice is terse.

Gabriel's smile spreads wide.

Raguel shifts in his seat, looking bored. "Four hundred souls have been granted to the Deacon." He waves. "You will return to your cell."

"She will not!" Gabriel stands. "The agreement has been satisfied. She is to go free."

Raguel frowns. It seems I am still valuable to him. He doesn't want to let me go. "She violated the terms when she escaped the Scarecrow."

Gabriel stands and points. "That wasn't specified in the deal."

"Did Gabriel's abomination fulfill her end of the agreement?" Raguel folds his hand on the table as he says, "Let's vote."

Five hands lift into the air on "Yay."

Bastards.

Two hands lift into the air on "Nay."

Raguel looks down his angelic nose at me as the shackle unclasps and moves away from my neck. "I suggest your tainted hide—"

"Oh, shut up," Gabriel bellows as he and Sparrow step down from the raised platform and walk toward me. "We're done here." Gabriel motions for me to move.

I walk out of the Babylon courthouse with my chin lifted in the air as the Angel spectators whisper and stare.

"Don't mind them," Gabriel says to me as he shoves the double doors open with force.

"I usually don't." Still, having them see me at my worst and most vulnerable makes me dislike them even more. Yet, I feel so free walking out of that courtroom. I didn't schlep it through five hundred yards of sewage like Andy Dufresne for this redemption, but between Heaven and Hell, it was pretty damn close.

THE SUNLIGHT of Heaven is bright, so bright.

I shield my eyes.

Sparrow hisses. His leathery wings snap open and extend over his head, shading his face from the sun.

"Is it that bad, boy?" Gabriel asks.

The Angels of Babylon are watching Sparrow. When he was a Legion Commander they viewed him with awe, now they shy away, a few actually run with their children crying in fear.

Monsters don't frequently walk here out in the open, or at least not with their true skin showing.

An attempt to vanquish a curse, he has been spread beyond simple good and evil. This is how nightmares and dark fairytales are born, a creature like Sparrow at the center of it. Where do I fit in? I flutter back and forth between it all, never taking an oath to either side, only to Sparrow.

"You don't belong here!" someone yells.

A tomato hurtles through the air and hits Sparrow on his thigh.

"Go back to Hell!" A rock flies through the air and hits me on the cheek, just grazing the skin but it's enough to draw blood.

Sparrow takes two steps before leaping into the air with a growl, headed toward the group of Angels who dare to threaten us.

Using my sleeve, I stop the bleeding.

I lean toward my father and ask, "Was it like that for you?" I tip my head toward Sparrow. "Were you nearly a different person?"

"Unfortunately." Gabriel frowns. "Time as a Hellion spares no Angel's original form or mindset." He pats his chest; "I was quite holy and proper before my time down there."

I come to the realization, connecting the speculation of my father being a bit crazy as well; it's just a cover to hide the dark things he's encountered. If only the inhabitants of this plane understood the path the Archangels trudged through so that they can live in this place, safe and sound.

Sparrow is hovering over the group of Angels, hissing and roaring. He lands; hiding his face with his leathery wings only to pop them open again with a peek-a-boo gesture that's sure to cause some pants to be soiled.

"How long was your term as a Hellion?" I ask.

"It varies for each family. Sparrow must work off his father's term as well as his own." Gabriel turns and frowns. "You should get him out of here before he hurts someone." He walks away abruptly ending our conversation.

One of the Angels scream.

I run toward Sparrow, jumping to grab him by the crook of his arm and pulling him until his feet are on the ground again.

"Come on," I say. "You can't be barking at the locals like this. We're going to get in even more trouble than we already are."

Thinking of where we can go to hide—*Poof*—We're at Sparrow's house in Gabriel's Kingdom.

Sparrow glances around and seems uneasy.

"This is your house," I remind him.

His lip curls and he shivers. "It's very... light. I don't remember it being this light."

I head for his radio and press the power button. Bon Jovi's greatest hits loads and *Runaway* starts playing. I turn to face Sparrow again.

He's staring at the bookshelf on the far side of the room. There's a row of books missing. I feel guilty for Birds of Paradise being lost to Hell, along with the rest of the books in the series. I could *poof* back and get them real quick, but I don't trust that I won't get stuck there and I don't want to leave Sparrow's side now that I've got him alone.

I move to the windows and close the blinds, trying to make it as dark as possible in the living room.

"Will you love me forever?" Sparrow suddenly asks.

I stop what I'm doing and turn to face him. He's standing in the shadows now, one column of light from the partially open blinds brightens his shoulder.

"Yes. Of course." I can only hope to, even with all the changes. He is the only one who has ever showed me love and caring and truth. How could I not love him forever?

Still, this feels wrong. What are we doing here in Heaven?

"Where will you go, Meg?" Sparrow tips his head to the side, a birdlike motion he used to make so much.

"They don't want me in Heaven." My father will be disappointed that I won't be staying here. "But I don't feel safe here. Not with Raguel and those five Archangels wanting me locked up."

"Come back with me," Sparrow offers as he holds his open hand out for me to take. "We don't belong here any longer, Meg."

I dwell on the proposition for a moment. Go back to Hell? I'm not safe there either. Lucifer and Clea will lock me up in that room and I'll go back to being Sparrow's Hungry Man dinner. I glance at him. But if I went back to Hell, we'd be together. And they all keep saying, "we'll be invincible together." I haven't seen an inkling of that yet; seems the only thing Sparrow and me get into is trouble.

"I think I'll go back to the Earthen plane," I decide.

Sparrow nods at my decision. "I'll go with you. For a little bit, then I must return to Lucifer's side."

Do I want him there? I'm not sure how much of this coming and going I can take. Do I let him come with me or do I send him packing? We want to be together but the laws of the ethereal realms keep tearing us apart.

Who am I kidding? I'm selfish as they come. I place my hand in his.

"Will you lead the way?" I ask, knowing that he can travel through realms just as easily as I can now.

The corner of his mouth tips up, as he replies, "You don't want to let me lead. If I decide, we'll end up locked in a cave in some dark place, where I can keep you safe and to myself for all eternity. I don't think you'd like that much."

I wouldn't. Not really at all. So I decide. I think I'll go back to Key West. The weather was nice and the ocean calming.

Poof.

We return to the Earthen plane.

I NOTICE AS SOON as we hit the beach that something strange is going on. Gunfire erupts in the distance, a pop-pop-pop-pop sound. There's shouting, smoke billowing in the air from fires burning. The burning buildings nearly mask the smell of death. I'd recognize that stench from a hundred miles away.

Sparrow looks at me, knowing.

Before all that bullshit of trading souls for my freedom, I was here and someone was dropping zombies in my general vicinity. I remember the news playing at Jed's tattoo shop, the zombie taking a bite out of that reporter.

Oh no.

The zombie apocalypse is full-bore.

Now, I don't give a sweet goddamn about much, but this, yeah, this I do. The Earthen plane was my home for much longer than either one of the ethereal realms. At least there's meaning behind the zombies of Hell, but they don't belong on here. I have to figure this out.

"How is this happening?" I ask Sparrow.

"We didn't send them," he replies.

"Who is *we*?" I know all too well that there are differing forces on each plane, groups always fighting for power.

"Myself, the Hellions, we are not responsible for this mess," Sparrow assures me.

Two of the dead are ambling across the beach, headed in our direction. Sparrow has his blade out. I pull mine from my thigh holster.

"You stay here," Sparrow says. "I'll get them."

"No." I step next to him as he advances. "We do this together. I'm not some pansy in need of saving."

Sparrow glances at me. "You're definitely not."

After the rotting bodies have been laid to rest, we walk toward town. The windows are smashed out of my beloved Sal's Bar. I enter the building, broken glass crunching under my boots. There's brain splatter on the wall and headless bodies still sitting in the booths. I step behind the counter and find two glasses that are intact and look clean. I turn and search Sal's stock for something strong, selecting a full bottle of Devil's Springs vodka, completely appropriate. I pour us each a half a glass.

"Cheers." I clink Sparrow's glass with mine.

We down the vodka and set our glasses on the bar. Just as we do a black feather flutters down between our glasses.

Now, Sparrow's always been enamored with feathers, never been able to keep his hands off one. He reaches out, his Hellion reflexes faster than I've ever seen. I move my hand quick, slapping it down trying to stop him; we wind up touching the thing at the same time. An arc of electricity extends between our fingertips. I see his pupils go pinpoint just as I'm sure he sees mine do the same.

And then... nothing.

No vision, no blackout, no falling unconscious and waking days later.

Sparrow starts humming, "Take Me Home Tonight."

When I look out the busted front window of the bar, there's a swarm of the dead waiting for us.

"You ready for this?" Sparrow asks.

"You bet your ass I am."

We ready our blades as we step over broken glass, advancing on the horde of the dead who belong less on the earthen plan than we do.

Bang a Gong

"Will you stay with me?" I ask, kissing Sparrow's cheek above a smudge of dirt.

He grips my hips, pulling me down against his groin. "Until the day breaks and the shadows flee away, I will, Meg. I'll stay with you."

I miss the days when we were nothing but human. Free to explore at will, just the two of us surviving, learning to trust each other.

Someone outside on the street screams, followed by the pop-pop-pop of gunshots. I try to block out the noise and focus on the man underneath me but the magic of the moment is lost.

"We should head out." I roll off him and find my clothes.

The dead on the earthen plane are always awake and ready to party. They don't sleep at night like the ones in Hell do. Which means there's no avoiding them at night. This is a twenty-four hour cleansing.

"Do you think they help?" Sparrow asks as I'm pulling my shirt on. "The runes?"

I twist my forearms and glance at the tattoos Jed gave me. "Funny thing about that, they only work if the Angels or Demons or whatever are looking for me don't already know what my face looks like."

Sparrow's tying his boots; he double-knots the laces before standing.

"Sometimes, I wonder," he steps toward me, "what your skin looked like before the tattoos."

"Had you stuck around—" I stop myself, knowing that bringing up the past of him leaving his Legion Commander post is a dark memory loaded with guilt.

He bends to collect my jacket off the floor. "We should get moving."

Just as I'm reaching for the door handle, the floorboards outside our room groan. Sparrow holds his hand up to pause me. There could be one of the dead out there. Or it could be a survivor. We haven't run into many here on the island, just a few who we've packed into cars and trucks and sent to the airport or the Coast Guard or Naval stations.

Sparrow suggested we search every house of worship and every graveyard on the island before moving on to Stock Island, slowly making our way through the islands of Key West by way of US route 1. Sparrow is keeping his eye out for the supernatural, anything that might tell us why this is happening here. Since I'm too much of a noob, I've caved and let Sparrow lead the way. He knows things that I don't about the ethereal realms. Or at least, I trust that he does.

Thankfully the government seems to be controlling most of the situation. There's still electricity in most parts of town, the running water works, CNN is giving live updates from all the cities with what they're calling "outbreaks of an unknown virus."

The gunshots we heard a little bit ago mean that there's more of the uninfected. The urge to help is strong. Sparrow's hand is hovering over the door.

"Open up. We know you're in there," an authoritative voice demands.

We've been avoiding the National Guard for obvious reasons. But they've been on our tail, noticing us running into alleyways as they're clearing the streets of corpses and delivering headshots to the undead. They want the island cleared of inhabitants just as much as we do, but we're on a mission.

Sparrow's palm opens, hovering over the door as someone on the other side bangs the butt of their gun against it in an angry knocking. He turns to me, shaking his head from side to side. It's time to make like a ghost and *poof* our way out of here. I take Sparrow's hand, we glance around the room to make sure we've got everything—*poof*—we're out of there.

ONE OF THE walking dead runs toward us, jaws snapping and grimy fingers grabbing. Sparrow is quick to release his blade and in one swift movement he chops the head off before turning to me and saying, "Nice choice."

I throw my hands in the air. "I can't see what's going on before I *poof*. Would you have rather stayed back there and been arrested?"

"They might not have arrested us." Sparrow sheathes his blade.

I laugh. "Right. Look at us." I motion to his leather clothing. "We scream trouble. It bleeds from our pores."

Sparrow flashes a smile. "You've always been trouble."

The air takes a certain charge. The salty wind blows my short hair up and around my head, creating a strange halo of darkness.

"What was that?" Sparrow turns.

"The wind."

He starts walking. "Not the wind."

Thunder cracks in the afternoon sky. Sparrow's spine goes straight.

"Thunderstorms roll in every afternoon here," I remind him. "It's nothing."

We walk down an empty street; bullet casings and blood stain the pavement. Lightning strikes in the distance. The seagulls are absent from the sky as the storm rolls in. I know from living here that a storm blowing in off the gulf could last five minutes or a few hours.

"Ah," Sparrow starts walking faster, "the church."

The Basilica of St. Mary Star of the Sea is our second to last search. We've been to all the other houses of worship on this island with no answers.

I stand outside the building; the beige brickwork and lack of elevation seem unimposing unlike many of the churches in upstate New York with their gothic architecture and dark gray stone.

Daddy always said I'd burn to a cinder if I ever stepped foot in a church. Wasn't my real daddy, of course, that was John Lewis. God damn his devil soul.

Sparrow motions for me to follow him along the walkway between the church and gardens. There are large floor to ceiling

French doors that have been left open to allow the sea breeze to cool the building. Sparrow pauses against the wall, tips his head and glances around before stepping inside.

Something is off, there is more than just the metallic tang of blood on the streets that's easy to ignore. My mouth floods with saliva. There is a lot of blood here. Somewhere. Fresh. And that pool of darkness in my soul wants a sip of it.

I glance at Sparrow. He's standing still between the pews, watching me.

"What?" I ask, annoyed.

"There are answers here," he says, cryptic if anything. He turns and makes his way to the altar.

There's something about a church, the air of worship and adoration, tears of loss and decades of hope all smashed into this space. All for what? A God that the humans don't even know exists.

A shiver slides up my back.

Of course He doesn't exist.

"Meg?" Sparrow is standing at the altar. "I think you should see this."

I make my way to his side, gripping onto his arm and pressing my hand over my mouth when I see what he's discovered.

There is what seems to be the remains of a priest, the black clothing is shredded, bits of flesh hang from bone and mostly blood remains. A thick, gooey, delicious puddle of blood. There's splatter on the back of the altar and the wall, the tabernacle.

Oh, I can't do this.

I run out of the church, the monster inside of me begging for me to drop to the floor and lick the pool of blood off the granite altar. I've tasted the blood of an Archangel, the urge to taste the blood of a true lamb of God is hard to ignore.

I cross the threshold of the French doors, over a cobblestone path, until my feet sink into grass. I'm in a garden; stonework here and there, a gated Our Lady of Lourdes grotto. I notice a headstone of coral rock scripted with: In Memory of the Unborn.

There was a time in my life, before shit got real fucked up, when I was pregnant with a child. I didn't know my fiancée was the son of a demon living on the Earthen plane, heck, I didn't know what I was truly a product of. But Jim seduced me, knocked me up and forever changed my life. But my child was never born. Jim and the Hellions made sure of this. Her soul rests in Hell as a snowy owl. Clea said she is two-thirds darkness and one-third light, the brightest light in the darkest of places. I wanted to name her Elise.

Now I'm staring at the headstone, In Memory of the Unborn.

Elise. This can't be a coincidence.

I shake my head and consider running as far away from this place as I can. My heart speeds up, my throat feels thick.

I'm good at running away. We all know this.

Sparrow is at my side before I make a decision. "Stay with me, Meg."

I glance up at him. He blinks, the green of his irises replaced with the torrid flames of Hell.

Something is happening.

Sparrow turns me to face him. He touches my arm, my waist. I grip his shoulder with one hand, the side of his neck with the other. We are holding on tightly to each other, the only thing keeping us both grounded and in control at the moment.

"I think..." Sparrow's voice is strained. "I think something is hunting us."

I'm trying not to follow my instincts. It's hard being surrounded by temptations. My first urge is to flee, to run and to hide. But... *my Sparrow*. I'm so tired of losing and leaving him. I'm so tired of being forced away. He is mine and I am his, and I've about had it with forces trying to keep us apart.

I need a moment to clear my head, to form a plan.

I have to protect Sparrow.

I give in, just for a moment or two.

Poof—I return to Jed's parlor where I got the tattoo and the runes, bringing Sparrow along with me.

Sparrow blinks as our surroundings change completely. "I could barely hold on," he says before dropping to the floor.

The tattoo shop is dark, only a few candles illuminate the shop. I feel frozen in place. Glancing down, I see that we have landed in the middle of some strange archaic design painted on the floor.

There's a noise near the front desk.

"Jesus," Jed says. "Meg. What are you doing here?" He rounds the desk and makes his way to us, grabbing a towel off a counter before dropping to his knees outside of the large circular hieroglyphs on the floor.

"What is this?" I ask.

"Sorry," he starts scrubbing at a circular portion of the painting, breaking the spell. "Hurry," he motions for us to move.

Sparrow and I step out of the rune before Jed brushes ink over the portion he scrubbed away.

"I just had to be safe." Jed runs across the room and peeks out the closed blinds. "Nothing followed you?"

"I can't guarantee," I say.

Sparrow moves and straightens his back, bringing him to his full height.

"Whoa." Jed looks up. "You're different from the last time I saw you."

Sparrow sniffs the air. "And you are..." Before he finishes, Sparrow advances on Jed, blade drawn.

Jed runs. He barricades himself behind the counter, a tipped over filing cabinet and chair his only protection. Holding one palm out, Jed whispers words similar to prayer. A white light emerges from his hand, holding Sparrow at bay.

"Sparrow!" I shout. "Stop. He can help us."

Sparrow's eyes flash to a bright green, reminding me of when I first met him. "He is an abomination and must die."

I already know that Jed is a forbidden creature. I wonder if this was part of Sparrow's duty as a Legion Commander in Gabriel's Kingdom, kill all the forbidden creatures?

"We are all abominations," I remind Sparrow. "Please," I touch his arm, "he can help us."

Sparrow finally lowers his blade in a reluctant motion. "If you say so."

"He helped me," I say. That seems to be enough to convince Sparrow that we can trust Jed.

Jed circles Sparrow. "You're kind of a big guy. A dark force. You're going to need a lot of ink."

Sparrow growls. "If you fuck with me, I will skin you. Sternum to toes."

Jed's eyes go wide.

"You'll have to excuse him," I say. "He's forgotten all of his manners since he became a Hellion."

Metal clangs as Jed drops his pot of ink. "A Hellion?" He

suddenly seems nervous. "We're going to need a lot more ink. And, perhaps a little blood."

"Use Meg's," Sparrow says as he takes his leather vest off. "I don't trust anyone else's." He lays on his stomach across a padded table.

Jed preps his skin, his entire back, right down to the low-rise of his leather pants.

"This better not hurt," Sparrow mutters.

"It's not going to tickle," I warn.

Jed dips the needle of his gun in a pot of ink starts working freehand. I watch from the opposite side of Sparrow as Jed shades the runes on Sparrow's skin. Every now and then Jed whispers a spell as he's working, or he sprinkles black dust on the fresh ink before blotting it with the towel and checking his work.

The last two times I met Jed, the lights dimmed and a blue aura shone around him. This time it didn't. I ask why.

"Because of this," Jed points to a fresh mark on his inner arm. "It's a new rune that hides the light from… you."

I feel a bit insulted. "Why me?" I cross my arms and lean back in my chair.

"I can't trust anyone. Not even a girl who can flash between realms and slay the walking dead like she was born and bred to take on the apocalypse single handedly."

"She won't do it alone," Sparrow speaks up. "We do it together."

"Isn't that special?" Jed dips the needle in ink and continues.

Jed updates us on the status of the zombie apocalypse in New York State as he works. We tell him what we've seen in Key

West. Minus what we saw at the church, I'm saving that for later.

During a moment of silence, Sparrow begins a conversation, asking Jed about his background, different spells and runes, otherworldly creatures and beings that I've never heard of before.

I try to absorb as much as possible. But after traveling across the country and trying to control myself around the massacre in St. Mary's, I'm exhausted. I close my eyes.

You left without saying goodbye, Nightingale is in my dream.

I open my mouth to apologize but nothing comes out. I should have known better, she never lets me talk during these visits.

The baby is in her arms nursing. Part of me is jealous of her getting to experience motherhood in all its loveliness.

You'll get your time again, Nightingale says when she notices me watching the baby. She looks off in the distance. "Jack is nice. He's not Noah, but he'll do. You should see him waiting on me hand and foot, bringing me food and checking on me, he's so nervous. Your father took him to Babylon to meet the Council." Nightingale blinks slowly and smiles. "I do like him." She sighs, switching the baby to her other breast to feed. "I can't find Noah in the Astral. I know. I know you'd tell me to leave him alone. He'd say the same, but... I miss him." She toys with the edge of her flowing top for a moment. "The reason I'm here," she clears her throat, "Teari wanted me to warn you. She was with Gabriel in Babylon and a Deacon was there. There's something strange happening, the viscera between realms is thinning. The Council is up in arms over what's happening on the Earthen plane. They're waiting for their message from God to intervene. I know you don't believe, Meg, but maybe now is a good time to find a little faith?"

I shake my head.

Nightingale makes a face.

I feel a sharp pain in my mouth. My tongue touches my front tooth, it wiggles loosely.

"Maybe you've got scurvy," Nightingale suggests. "All these dreams of your teeth falling out in handfuls. Maybe you should eat an orange or a lime, suck on something besides my brother's neck for a change. Teari says it might do you good." The baby moves its hand in a swatting motion and starts to fuss. "I named him Thrush." Nightingale purses her lips and delivers a cheerful trilling song, rushed and jumbled. Thrush smiles up at his mother. "Tell Noah something for me." Nightingale looks up. "Anything." And then she's gone.

I WAKE and peek at Sparrow and Jed from partially opened eyelids. First it was Clea and Gabriel, now Noah and Nightingale. I wonder if the same fate of love lived apart is the destiny I share with Sparrow? We've spent plenty of time apart, on different realms, but it gets harder each time.

Jed sits back, his shoulders and neck crack as he stretches. He's been working on Sparrow's back for hours. The runes are detailed, beautifully intricate, stretching the length of the base of Sparrow's skull to the dimple in his lower back. I lick my lips. Sparrow's always *done it* for me, but seeing him like this, inked up like me, it makes something deeper than my trailer park roots quiver.

"Have you heard of the ouroboros?" Sparrow asks Jed.

"The serpent who eats its own tail. Why do you want to know about that?"

"Tell me."

"The serpent eats its own tail to sustain its life. An eternal cycle of renewal."

Sparrow glances at me.

I give up on fake-sleeping and open my eyes. I rub my thumb over the mark on my thigh, which is covered by my jeans. I don't think I'd ever eat my own tail, not that I have a tail. And I don't have memories of a life before this one. I guess there are no simple answers to my birthmark.

Jed keeps working on Sparrow's ink while I pace the shop. I peek out the windows. Every so often a zombie ambles by or a group of National Guardsmen. They pay no attention to the tattoo shop.

"Meg," Jed calls. "It's time for the blood."

I walk to where he's holding out a small metal dish. Using my blade, I slice my wrist and let it drip until Jed says he has enough.

Sparrow's eyes zero in on the cut. I offer him my wrist. There is the sharp pinch of his teeth, followed by a gentle tugging of him drinking. Jed is watching. I feel dirty. This is kind of intimate; I don't like having a third party watching.

Jed dips his needle in the blood and continues.

The fresh tattoos on Sparrow's back heal instantly after he's fed from me.

Jed backs away, taking in what just happened.

I turn away, not looking to explain anything.

Jed dips his tattoo machine in the dish and continues.

Hours pass. I flip through the news channels and check the windows.

Jed sits back, admires his work on Sparrow's back. He touches up a few of the swirling runes before standing.

"We should get some rest for the night. I can touch this up in the morning," Jed offers. "Although, I'm certain this is perfect." He admires his work.

"Do you have anything to eat?" Sparrow asks.

"Wherever you two are going when you're done here, I'm not going with you. I can't give you the last of my food stock."

I press my hands to my stomach to control the grumble. "It's fine," I tell Sparrow. "We'll find something in the morning."

Sparrow and I sit with our backs to the wall. He puts his arm across my shoulders and I lean on him. Since I didn't get much rest with Nightingale's visit, I fall asleep.

I'M NOT sure where I find the energy for the filthy dream I'm in the middle of. Sparrow's stripped naked, looking like a beast with his tattoos and muscles flexing. I'm crawling toward him on my hands and knees. There are shackles around both of our necks. A voice laughs nearby, another moans. There are dark whispers as I reach Sparrow's feet and climb up his body. He's just watching me, irises aflame with the burning fires of Hell. All I can think of is my hunger and the impending zombie battle we must face in Key West. I want to be sated. I want to be strong. I bite down on Sparrow's neck, his arms circle around my back and grip my ass. Feathers are falling from the sky, someone is whispering faster and faster. Thick blood fills my mouth and I swallow it down, taking my fill. Guzzling. The shackle around my neck tightens.

I am so tired of being controlled. I want to be *free*.

My eyes flash open.

It's not Sparrow's muscular body I've been feeding from.

It's Jed's.

OH SHIT. Oh shit, shit, shit, shit. I move to my feet and back away. Did I kill him? I think I might have killed him…

"He's still alive." Sparrow is sitting on the other side of the room, watching.

I feel sick.

What did I just do?

It wasn't so long ago that I had no qualms against two-timing and doing whatever I wanted. But Sparrow's the first guy who I'd never want to hurt in that way. And now I'm such a hypocrite, forbidding Sparrow from feeding off the Blood-whores, and now I go and do this!

"If you were that hungry, you could have told me. I'd never let you starve, Meg."

My heart cracks. "I'm sorry."

"No reason to be sorry. You didn't suck his dick."

My face flames red. "Holy hell, you're not supposed to say things like that."

"I can say what I want." He moves to his feet and makes his way to me. "Let me taste, and I'll tell you whose son he really is."

Sparrow dips his head and licks a drop of blood from the

corner of my mouth. "Mmm." He thinks for a moment. "Nephelium of the Archangel Michael. It's amazing that he's lived this long without being found. The runes must work quite well." Sparrow lifts Jed as though he was light as a feather, and sets him upright in a chair to recover.

"You can tell all of that from a taste of blood?" I did feel stronger when I drained Remiel dry; I felt insane power and control but that was it.

"Yes."

"And when you taste my blood?"

"Danger. Among other things." Sparrow moves close to me, until I can feel the heat from his body. "And when you taste mine, Meg?"

I think for a moment. "Lust." There's plenty of lust, a lot of lust, actually. I can barely keep my pants on when I feed from Sparrow.

I can't stand around talking about how Sparrow makes me feel.

"What do we do now?" I ask.

"We have to go back and face whatever is hunting us."

"I just want it to end, Sparrow. I want to be free from all of these *forces*." It's been a long time since I've felt the urge to give up completely.

"Meg?" Sparrow asks as he's pulling his vest on.

I want this to be on my terms.

"If we're going back, then I want to drive," I say.

"That's not exactly the quickest way."

I step toward Sparrow. "I know it's completely selfish of me to want you all to myself. But if something is hunting us, they'll find us sooner or later. We're just taking the scenic route back to Key West."

"This is really no time for a road trip."

"I'm not wasting my energy *poofing* us back there. Whoever or whatever is hunting us can just hurry up and wait." I reach up on my toes and kiss him. "They always said we'd be invincible together. So, let's be together."

Jed moves. His eyes slowly open.

"I'm sorry about that," I say.

"I may never forgive you," Jed croaks, his voice is hoarse and weak.

"We're leaving now."

"Don't be offended if you come back here and the shop's closed up," Jed warns. "You won't find me again."

"It's probably better that way," Sparrow says.

"Just so you are aware, Meg, those runes cloak him from all, including you."

Sparrow

He'd never been on a road trip before. But this was nothing more than a means to an end. Sparrow knew that Meg knew that they didn't belong here. There was only one realm for them, which was becoming more and more apparent. No matter how much she loved her beloved Earthen plane, they couldn't stay. They had to end the walking of the dead and leave. But, Sparrow admitted to himself that he'd never seen a landscape as beautiful as the Blue Ridge Mountains as they drove Route 81 through Virginia and North Carolina. Meg had pulled over at least ten times on the way down the mountain to simply stare.

"It's breathtaking," she had said as she leaned over the wooden railing and took it all in. "Never saw anything like this in upstate."

Meg had turned the engine off but left the music on and Bon Jovi's *Bed Of Roses* was playing on the radio. She was wearing a short black dress and leather sandals. Sparrow blinked, a snapshot to commit to memory—she'd never be this calm again once she found out what he'd promised Lucifer. They watched the sunset, the low clouds rolled between the mountain peaks and the fading rays of sun lit her with a halo.

Sparrow could barely breathe. Meg was always a bundle of dark energy, one he could never keep away from, one he'd do anything to protect. But in this moment, she looked like an Angel. And he had to take the moment as his, every thread of his being begged to possess her. He couldn't control himself for one second. Sparrow hiked up the back of Meg's skirt and bent her over the railing.

"Oh," Meg moaned but didn't protest. She never did, she was as addicted to Sparrow as he was to her. He thrust into her hard, snaked one arm across her hips to hold her in place. His other hand moved across her front, between her breasts, to hold the side of her neck as she tipped her head. The sunlight filtered through her hair in amber and pale pink hues. It illuminated the watercolor tattoo of the sparrow on her chest.

She is mine, echoed through his head.

She angled her head, offering her pulsing jugular. He was greedy, taking her like this and not offering himself in return. The darkness that was squeezing Sparrow's soul didn't care; it would take what it wanted, when it wanted.

He thrust harder, Meg moaned louder. He wanted to strip her dress off and lay her bare on the rocks of the mountain.

The last rays of light disappeared behind the peaks, cloaking them in shadows. Sparrow was so dark in this transition of daylight, he knew he was no more that a shadow of a man. The car was hiding them from the road but if anyone happened to see them, they'd only see her, for this was the hour when dark things came out to play. Sparrow could see them slithering between the mountain peaks and dancing in the night fog. They didn't belong here. This was not their realm.

He thrust one last time, hearing the wooden railing groan in protest from the burden of their weight. He stopped himself from drinking his fill. He didn't want Meg weak. Having sated his dark beast, Sparrow pulled out, tugged her skirt down, and slapped her on the ass.

Meg turned and strung her arms around his neck. "Of all the dark dirty deeds, that has got to be the best." She smiled as she kissed him.

Sparrow regretted not having a mind full of memories of Meg in this state, shameless and nearly innocent. It was moments like this that Sparrow knew were few and far between. Now that everyone knew who they were, peace would be a goal they'd forever hunger for.

Sparrow wondered how long Lucifer would let this go on. He'd be called back eventually. Meg was sleeping in the passenger seat, her dark hair fluttering in the wind from the rolled down window.

Sparrow knew what was coming. He'd had a vision of it the day she was born. A vision that had caused him to flee. This would be the hardest time. They were invincible; they could be invincible, if she ever found her faith. They could lose everything, each other. Anticipation was a yo-yo in the back of his throat. And as much as he hated the prospect of losing her, he knew it was best to face this thing head on.

Sparrow closed his eyes and—*poof*—they were driving down I-75, just a few hours north of Tampa. They'd be in Key West by morning.

MEG

I wake to the sound of thunder rumbling. Looking out the window, I recognize the skyline.

We're in Florida.

I turn to face Sparrow. "How did we get here so fast?" I ask.

"You've been sleeping." He smiles and it's enough to pacify me.

I sit up and run my hands through my hair. That means I was sleeping for, like, *days*. Well, he did fuck my brains out at that rest stop. Maybe I needed to recover?

I reach into the back seat and grab a soda and bag of chips. The breakfast of champions. Nothing tastes better than the sugary syrup of an orange soda first thing in the morning. It's almost better than coffee.

We drive with the radio blaring an 80's throwback channel, until I-75 cuts across the Cypress preserve where there's nothing but fenced trees, a four lane road and blue skies dotted with puffs of cloud. We finally stop at a recreational area in the Everglades. It's nothing like what you see on TV, there's no swamp this close to the highway, no gators or giant mosquitoes. It actually reminds me of an old country road from where I grew up.

Sparrow parks the car under the shade of a short palm tree.

I get out and head for the bathroom.

Sparrow is leaning against the car, watching a flock of ravens caw back and forth to each other.

I push open the women's bathroom door, only to be greeted by four dead women, all who would rather eat my face instead of offer their empty bathroom stall.

I slam the door closed and run out of the rest stop building, barricading the door with a bench. I decide to use the bushes instead, and pray that a gator doesn't take a bite out of my ass.

As I'm walking up the incline and climb over the guardrail, I scan the parking lot and no longer see Sparrow propped against the car.

Oh no! "Sparrow!" I shout.

Suddenly I see him taking quick strides across the parking lot and catching a large black feather that's fallen from one of the ravens.

But he wasn't there a second ago. There was nothing, I was alone.

A man is walking across the parking lot, headed toward me. I grip my blade, but pause. The man doesn't have the jagged walk of the dead, and his clothing look clean and pressed. He walks with a straight back and clear eyes.

I recognize him. It's Reuben.

Reuben stops in front of me. He looks so nice and normal, just like that day I stepped into his office looking for a lawyer. I blink a few times to make sure I'm not dreaming.

"How did you find us?" I ask.

"You're in Florida now." He points at a white pole with four camera bulbs encased in tempered glass. "There are cameras on every highway. This is not that po-dunk town you grew up in. Those marks on your arms will only hide you for so long. All it takes is one minion to recognize your face on the camera footage."

Just perfect. "What are you doing here?"

"I've come to provide counsel."

"You're no longer my lawyer." I grip my blade, eager to end him.

"I may not be, Meg. But we're on the Earthen plane again, and I'm no longer taking orders from the powers above me. We were friends before I had to take you in."

I think I need to reconsider the meaning of the word *friend*.

I glance at Sparrow in the distance.

"He's been a fallen angel, a Legion Commander returned, a Hellion, Lucifer's right hand, and now... what is he?"

I am silent.

"He doesn't even know. And neither do you."

"What's your point?"

"I come here with a warning—"

"I've got a warning for you, Reub. Go fuck yourself." I walk away from him and head toward Sparrow.

When I turn around again, Reuben is gone.

As I walk up behind Sparrow, he's humming *Two Tickets to Paradise*.

"Where'd you go just now, Sparrow?" I ask.

"Didn't go anywhere, Meg," he replies with that tone of blind innocence that I haven't heard in so long. He shoves the raven feather in his pocket. He turns and grins at me.

There are no differences between friends and enemies, my grandfather once told me. But Sparrow is much more than a friend to me.

A helicopter buzzes overhead. The authorities are probably searching for hordes of the dead that need to be put down.

"We should get moving," I suggest. "Before the noise brings more of the dead. I want to drive."

I get in the driver's seat. Sparrow sits next to me. Meatloaf starts playing on the radio. Sparrow's tapping his foot before he breaks into song, "...never had a girl looking better than you..."

I shift the car into gear and sing the lyrics of that strange lady in the white jumpsuit, remembering the last time we sang a duet together in a car as free as two jays in the brush, headed for the unknown.

―――――

When I was living in Key West, I never left the island, this drive has got me wishing I had. There's nothing but blue sea and blue sky and a stretch of pavement. Heaven is heaven, but this... this is heaven to me.

Sparrow's humming "Never Say Goodbye" since the radio signal dropped out just south of Miami.

Thankfully the National Guard is busy clearing the streets and keeping the dead at bay. We pass one barricade in which the Guard let us through with barely two glances. He probably figures we either know what we're doing or if we're stupid enough to enter then we're better off dead.

―――――

I park the car in front of The Basilica of St. Mary Star of the Sea. The air remains charged like before. The sky darkens and this time I conclude that it is more than just a Gulf storm blowing in.

We get out of the car.

"I think I should get backup for this," Sparrow suggests.

"Where would you get that?"

"I could cross realms and collect Skeele, or a few of the other Hellions."

I'm afraid if he goes, he'll never return. "You and me, we can do this together."

"In a blaze of glory," he says as he rounds the car and walks to my side. "If you insist."

We cross the street and enter the grounds of St. Mary's by the walkway on the southwest side of the building.

Sparrow inhales deeply. "It's still here."

We enter the church through open French doors, both gripping our blades. Sparrow walks between the pews. I walk along a wall of stained glass depicting the seven Archangels. Their images look nothing like they do in real life.

"Meg," Sparrow calls me to the altar.

I make my way to him, unease in my gut. I can smell the blood. The slaughtered priest is still there.

"I think you should taste it," Sparrow says.

"You taste it." I curl my lip in disgust.

Neither of us moves.

"If you were hunting us," I say. "How would you set the trap?"

"Draw us in with what we desire most." Sparrow turns. He pulls the raven feather from his pocket, dips it in the preacher's blood and tastes it.

So now he uses feathers as a utensil? My Sparrow Man never ceases to surprise me.

Sparrow frowns. "It's not here." He moves toward another one of the open French doors, leading us to the side garden.

A snowy owl swoops out of the gated Our Lady of Lourdes grotto and lands on the headstone. *In Memory of the Unborn.*

Elise?

The owl hoots once before disappearing like a ghost.

We've done this before. Sparrow collected his feathers from the snowy owl a long time ago. That's an old desire. But a child, my child, that's a desire I'm unsure of, I'm not ready for.

This is a distraction.

"We will be invincible together," Sparrow whispers the phrase like a mantra. "We will be invincible together. We will be invincible together. We will be invincible together."

"Are you nervous or something?" I ask. A man as dark and scary as him shouldn't be frightened at this moment. Should he?

Sparrow doesn't answer.

I try to focus.

What do we desire most?

Sparrow makes his way to the grotto. I follow, gripping my blade tighter.

There is a fountain made of cobblestone and etched with familiar runes.

Sparrow touches the rock. "It's a portal."

"To where?" I ask. "It's water."

"Universal conduit." He steps back.

I dip my fingers in the water.

"Don't, Meg," Sparrow warns.

Too late. The water bubbles rapidly. Steam rises. The ground rumbles. A black beak pokes through, followed by black beady eyes. But like Pinocchio's nose when he tells the truth, they dissipate to the face to a man. The face of Reuben.

"Hey Meg," Reuben says—a bit too cheery—as he steps out of the fountain and onto the ground of the grotto. "Nice seeing you again."

"Scarecrow." Sparrow's blade presses against Reuben's chest. "You should not be here. She is free of your hold."

"I've come to deliver a message."

I turn to leave the cover of the grotto, my hand on Sparrow's arm. "I have no desire to listen to you." All that time he dragged me around Hell, finding Jack and getting him to repent at the Safe House, Reuben may have been taking orders but he was cruel.

Reuben says, "Let me explain something—"

"You get to explain nothing!" I threatened to kill him a long time ago. I should have then. "Your people have already used me to collect hundreds of souls."

We step out of the grotto and onto the manicured grounds of the church.

Reuben follows. "You need to listen to me."

"I collected Jack. I paid my penance to Babylon for killing Remiel. I'm free of this."

"But don't you want answers?"

No. I want to find a bar and a hotel with clean sheets and a hot shower. "Go away," I tell him.

"What kind of answers?" Sparrow asks.

"The dead are walking on the Earthen plane for a reason," Reuben says.

"That reason." Sparrow secures his blade at his hip and crosses his arms over his chest like he's settling in for a long conversation.

"Your last bit of grace is disrupting the fiber between Hell and the Earthen plane. You've spent too much time down there."

Sparrow frowns as he ponders what Reuben is saying.

"There's only one thing to do," Reuben says as he turns to me. "You have to take that last piece of light left in his soul. You must do it, Meg. You must *kill* him." Reuben points at Sparrow.

I've killed plenty in my day, more than I ever though I would. But not him. Never him. "No. No. No. No. No!"

"Come on," Reuben says as he slaps his thighs in a motion of objection. "He won't really be dead. You'll just kill that last speck of Angel inside of him. Extinguish that light. He's ruining *everything*."

I don't get to ask what exactly everything is because Sparrow grabs my hand and turns me to face him. He moves my arm and positions my blade against his heart. He circles his hand over mine.

"No," I whisper, eyes wide and heart breaking. "This isn't right."

"What's right? This all started with me not following the rules. I abandoned my post. I spread a curse upon my family. I altered your destiny. I've brought the dead walking upon the Earthen plane."

Sparrow has been marinating in shame, all this time, he's never let it go.

"There has to be another way," I say.

"Nope," Reuben speaks up. "This is the only way."

"We must end this. Help me end it, Meg." He pushes my blade deeper into his chest, past the resistance of bone.

"No." I shake my head but grip the blade tighter. That Sparrow who I first met will never be again.

"They always warned me that you'd break my heart," he says with a sad smile. "I should've seen it coming when the roses died."

Tears sting my eyes. "I never wanted to."

"This ain't a lovesong," he sings the lyrics to his favorite songs in a deep crooning.

Sparrow's wings are suddenly visible. They snap out; encircle him, tight like a cocoon. I step back. A tiny speck of light rises out of the tip, it hovers in the air spurting light like a sparkler on the fourth of July, before it smolders to nothing.

"Don't forget me, Sparrow." A tear slides down my cheek. "The things they've made me do."

Sparrow's veins turn black, up his neck and to his ears. He roars a deafening sound. A sepia light burns, outlining the runes tattooed on his back.

He's your monster now.

That fear I felt the first time the Hellions stormed my home resurfaces. I never wanted to see Sparrow in that dim light, but right now, I can't help it.

"Congratulations," Reuben says. "You've upset the balance. Let a monster lose upon the Earthen plane. It's so far gone now that you're going to pay."

What the fuck?

"The Deacons made me do it," Reuben says with a guilty smile.

"You're the worst kind of asshole." I reach for my blade and relieve his head from his shoulders.

Reuben's head and body drop to the ground with a plop. That was satisfying.

Something cinches in my gut.

A tight feeling like a fist grabbing my insides. It tugs, pulls, yanks me back. I claw at the air as I am dragged backward, into the shadows, into the darkness of the grotto, through the water portal that soaks me to the bone, only to be deposited inside some dark dwelling, so dark I can't see a thing.

What have I done?

Stand There and Watch Me Burn

I've decided, I'm going to slay every last Deacon. Every single one. When I get out of this dark, dank place I'm going to hunt them down. Maybe I'll make a necklace from their teeth. Maybe I'll skin them all and dance around in their hides. Whatever I do, it's going to be epic, and final. They are the gray murkiness that slithers between realms without breaking rules. They must be ended. I will eradicate every last Deacon on every plane, if it's the last thing I ever do.

Fingers snap, a pale light flickers in the darkness.

"Hello?" I ask.

Things are slithering. The sound of rough skin and scales sliding against each other is nearly deafening.

The light gets brighter.

"Who's there?"

"Is that you, Meg?" I recognize Noah's voice.

"Noah!" I reach toward the light. "Noah! It's me."

His face comes into focus.

I'm not sure how long I've been in this darkness, but it's

been long enough that the presence of a friend brings sudden joy and hope.

"Meg, I'll never understand how you manage to get yourself in such deep shit."

"I didn't do anything." I shake my head.

"Bullcrap." Noah claps his hands together and light erupts. "You're lucky my Astral magic still works."

"Where are we?" I ask.

Something hisses.

"Since you're seeing this handsome face, you're back in Hell." He looks around us. "Somewhere in Hell."

Slither. Rattle.

I reach for my blade.

There is a hollow rattle, the snapping of jaws. The lamenting moans of eons of damned souls.

"That doesn't sound good," Noah warns. He uses his magic to increase our radius of light.

Two red eyes in the shadows illuminate.

"More light," I say, gripping the hilt of my blade.

He pushes the light, revealing a giant snake-like creature coiled in the shadows surrounding us.

"Ah!" Noah screams, high pitched like a cheerleader who's seen a spider. "What is that?"

"Jesus." I shove him away. "What good are you?"

The giant snake hisses and snaps at us.

"Please tell me you've got some magical bullshit up your sleeve to help with this?"

"Can't you just *poof* us out of here?" Noah asks.

Well, that's a good question. I take his hand and—

"Meg?" I recognize my mother's muffled voice.

"Clea?" I ask.

"Meg!" Her voice travels with the scaled slithering of the snake.

"I think she's inside that thing," Noah says.

"Help me," Clea cries.

I scan the snake's gut to try and pinpoint her voice. "Keep talking."

The snake's tail slithers, fast and intertwining, I can never quite find the portion where my mother's voice echoes. I slash at the thick skin. The snake hisses and its giant mouth descends on us.

"Noah, a little help."

Noah pushes a ray of light at the beast. It backs away, searching for another shadowy corner to attack from.

"Be careful," Clea's muffled voice warns.

I slice. A thick coil of the snake's body slams into us. I drop and roll but the belly of the snake is holding me down on the ground. I slice at it, my blade only making superficial nicks. I think I'm just pissing the creature off more.

Noah throws more rays of light and the snake slithers away.

"Can't you just light the entire place up?" I ask, annoyed.

"I can try." Noah claps his hands together, focuses, and a bright light erupts. The snake hisses as its skin smokes and burns.

"More," I urge.

"It can't survive in the light," Clea's muffled voice says.

Noah's eyes are squeezed shut as he creates brighter and brighter light. The snake's head snaps at Noah, trying to reach him around the light, it's body coiling and slithering over itself.

The snake moves for Noah, its large mouth descending on him. Wider and wider it opens, until in one snapping motion, it closes over Noah's figure. All is dark again.

The body of the snake shifts, releasing me from under its tough belly.

"Noah!"

Light radiates from between the snake's teeth, out of its nostrils, its head looks like it's glowing from the inside. The eyes bulge and in a strange popping sound, the entire head explodes into ash.

Noah is standing still, his palms bright with light.

"This kind of magic would have been nice weeks ago, manservant."

Noah shrugs in response. "This is all new to me."

"Help," Clea shouts.

We search the remaining snake's body, which twitches and slithers with death until we find a bulge.

"Hang on." I ready my blade, slicing the gut, deeper and deeper.

A pale arm reaches out. I grasp it and pull. Clea slides out of its gut.

"I hate it when he banishes me in there." The pale image of my mother shivers.

I do my best to wipe the goo off my arms.

Suddenly our reality shifts. We are no longer standing upright, the room tilts and we all drop.

"You killed my basilisk?" My grandfather stands from his desk, looking pissed.

"Daddy, that thing was disgusting." Clea is shaking slime from herself.

"Oh, dear sweet daughter, I wish you'd shut up for once." Lucifer's hand moves and a metal restraint clasps around Clea's mouth and back of her head. Her eyes go wide as she looks at me, shaking her head in silent warning.

What is it with these people and metal shackles?

Noah stills, recovering from his use of magic. His figure flickers in and out, threatening to send him back to the Astral to recover.

Lucifer kicks the headless body of the snake. "Now I'll have to catch another one." He turns to me. "Great job, Meg."

"For what?" I secure my blade on my hip and continue wiping the slime of the snake off me.

"You've released the greatest weapon I've ever owned," he replies.

I stand still, guessing that he's no longer talking about the giant snake that he kept in his ceiling.

"An Archangel who's lost all his grace now tattooed tailbone to scalp, unrecognizable to many. He's out there on the Earthen plane, collecting souls for me."

Sparrow?

"He's surpassed the four hundred that were stolen from me when your pal Jack escaped. But, now that Sparrow's promised me four terms, I'm sure he'll fill up the bowels of Hell in no time. I'll pay off the Deacons with more than double what the pesky Council paid them for Jack's soul. And then I win." Lucifer raises two fists, middle fingers pointed up at the heavens. "*I* win!"

I've never felt as sick as I do in this moment. My gut drops, saliva pools in my mouth threatening vomit, my knees go weak. What have I done?

"What in the name of God have you made me do?" I ask. I wouldn't bring him up, but it always seems to make these ethereal beings stand at attention.

Lucifer laughs. "There is no God. He left, so long ago."

"I don't believe you." But, I do believe him. Mostly because I don't believe in God.

"He was so disappointed in his sons and daughters that he left us for galaxies beyond. He left to create new and better worlds. He left us to wallow in misery and war. We failed him and he left *us*."

That's not what they told me in Heaven. "But everyone says that the Earthen plane—"

"They're wrong!" Lucifer slams his fists down on the desk. "The Earthen plane is *unruled*. The Angels have tried to protect it for eons, they don't want to believe the truth."

I glance across the room. Noah is watching warily while trying to use his newfound magic to release Clea from her bindings.

Lucifer continues, "And you were allowed to be birthed for one, singular reason. I will no longer be locked in Hell. Draining you will give me access to all. Half the human population has lost their faith, not even you believe in Him. That's all I need. Temptation and disbelief and they're all mine, they've already promised themselves to me. Sin is rampant. I just needed you to become stronger."

I shake my head. "You're wrong. Some power cast me out of the Earthen plane."

Lucifer's brows rise in interest. "That was me."

Maybe Jim never constructed that forbidden portal without Lucifer's knowledge. That trench I found Sparrow digging in was filled to the brim with bones. Those Hellions must have brought back hundreds of humans, stealing them away from the Earthen plane under the radar of the Angels. Maybe this was Lucifer's plan all along.

I wonder if Clea knew.

I pull my blade and point it at Lucifer. "Stay away from me."

He laughs, wicked and deep.

Noah does something that causes Clea's bindings to fall to the floor.

Lucifer growls. "It was a mistake to bring you back and tether you to her." He looks at me. "You see what weakness family brings? I should have left you huddling on the floor in fear that day."

I grip my blade. Lucifer circles me and I try my best not to have my back to him, but he moves so fast, a blur at times, weaving in and out of the shadows.

"Wingless queen. Nomad devil. Angel nevermore." His wings spread wide.

He bites me, with one quick suck of blood from my veins.

"Oh, granddaughter, you've been sampling royalty again. Did Michael tell you how I stood on his balls before he defeated me? If there was anything I learned from that battle, it was to embrace the darkness and release whatever angelic light was left inside me." He tips his head. "Just like Sparrow."

No! I run for him, dodge the sharp end of his blade, swipe my blade against his thigh. He roars and laughs, taunting.

"Such a little thing to take on the King of Hell." He moves as a blur, nicks my stomach, back and cheek. "Did your seagull of a father never teach you battle?" he mocks me.

I crouch, spin, and slice the back of his leg.

Clea is whispering words of magic.

The snowy owl suddenly swoops in through the window. Elise!

With one swift movement, Lucifer cuts her down the middle.

"No!" I scream.

Blood and feathers litter the ground. I was never the sentimental kind, but seeing the soul of my unborn daughter vanquished in front of me ignites a rage.

I don't get a chance to charge him.

Lucifer grabs my ankle and launches into the air and out the window, dangling me. "That ouroboros sealed your fate long before you knew it," he says. "This is where my kingdom gets to watch."

The ouroboros. *The serpent eats its own tail to sustain its life. An eternal cycle of renewal.* Could it be so simple and strange? *What would Andy Dufresne do?* Hide an escape behind a poster of a lustful woman. Could it be the answer?

I dangle upside down, gripped by my ankle, the tip of Lucifer's blade presses into my neck.

I bring my arm to my mouth, bite, suck my own blood.

Lucifer scowls with bewilderment.

I was never much into scripture, none at all, actually. But back at St. Mary's I read those inscriptions about the seven Archangels; Michael defeated Satan during a heavenly war, and his blood flows through my veins now since I fed from his child.

Strength comes.

I kick Lucifer's hand, knocking his blade away. I twist my body, grab his leg, crawl up his body like a spider, jab my blade into his gut. I accept for the moment that I am bred of monsters; I am a monster, bloodthirsty and damned. I bite my grandfather in the neck. He screams, his wings beat like two rugs being slapped together as he tries to shove me away with no success.

I use his technique, I embrace my darkness. Finally.

I suck a mouthful of his blood and swallow it down.

Lucifer roars a deafening howl of defeat. He shrivels under my hands, his wings still beating, still keeping us airborne, flying higher and higher into Hellsky. His giant frame withers, his leather clothing hangs off him as though he is nothing but bone.

I drain every last drop.

All life is gone as he releases me and drops from the sky. *Clank clank clank.* His hollow bones knock against the dirt of Hell.

"Meg!" Clea screams from the window of Lucifer's castle, Noah at her side, watching this spectacle.

I hover in the moment for a heartbeat. And then the gravity of Hell begs to collect my weight.

I drop to the ground like a sack of shit.

I hear Noah shouting over the sound of my bones breaking.

"The balance," Clea scolds as she holds him back.

What is it like to know that your daughter must die so not to upset the ethereal balance? I could never. But then, she tried to save me by distracting Lucifer, even if it was only for a second.

My skull hits the hard-packed dirt of Hell last.

Bright light, darkness.

My last thought is of my lost Sparrow.

He is mine and I am his.

But what are we without each other?

No Rest for the Wicked

"Meg?" Nightingale is skating around me. Thrush is giggling, secured on her back with a sling. "Oh Meeeeg?" She whistles a lively trill.

"What did she do?" Jack asks.

"She killed her grandfather." Nightingale whispers. "Meg!"

"Why would she do that?"

"Did Gabriel explain nothing to you?"

"He's very cryptic in his *explanations*. And he keeps flicking me in the forehead."

"That means he likes you." Nightingale skates faster. "Meg, wake up!"

I don't know where I'm going, but I know where I've been. That might be a Whitesnake quote. I'm definitely leaning toward a Whitesnake quote. Sparrow would be disappointed that I don't quote Bon Jovi.

I'm lost in my head. There is simply darkness, a warm embrace, coddling me like a womb.

I want Sparrow here.

Before, I could focus on a person and find them. That's how I found my mother when she was a bag of bones in the ground, that's how I found Sparrow when we were visiting his father.

I try to focus on Sparrow, but I can't. I can't find him.

The darkness gets darker. A black hole.

———

This heat is unbearable.

"Her bones are healing," Teari says.

I want to swat her away, but I can't move my arms.

"How much longer?" Gabriel's voice is gruff.

The whispering voices of the other Council members break through.

"I think you should just leave her the fuck alone," Jack says.

Right on, Jack. Leave me the fuck alone.

———

"Did she die for real?" Noah asks.

"No," Clea answers, her cold hand soothing my burning skin. "She didn't die." There is sadness in her voice. "Thank the heavens, she didn't die."

"Not even a little bit?" Noah asks.

"All or nothing. You should stock her fridge in case she wakes up," Clea suggests. "She's going to be hungry."

"That's a northern flicker," Noah says.

"No," Nightingale argues. "It's something else."

"It's not, we saw it in the book."

"Well go get the book and we can look it up."

"What book are you two talking about?" Jack asks.

"Birds of the Northeast," Nightingale replies. "Where is it?"

"I haven't seen it in a while," Noah says.

"Oh, wait," Jack says. "I think I know where it is."

Blessed silence as they all leave.

"What happened to this thing?" Nightingale asks.

"Fell out of the sky, almost smacked her in the face," Jack replies.

Crinkling pages turn.

"See?" Noah says, "It's a northern flicker. I told you so."

"Who cares?" Jack says.

Silence.

Awkward but blessed silence.

It doesn't last nearly long enough.

Nightingale says, "Jack, we're big into birds here. We all care. Just look at them." She whistles a short trill and a variety of birds answer her back in their own unique whistles and squawks and chirps. "They're precious."

"I don't understand," Jack says, unimpressed.

A baby giggles.

"Go ahead," Lucifer's voice suggests, "tug on my wishbone, see if you get the biggest shard and make your wish."

It's very tempting. What would I wish for? A buffet of snacks, sodas and chips. I'm hungry.

"Why don't you wake up, granddaughter? See what you did to me. See what you did to my kingdom."

"You're dead, so shut up."

"Dead to them." There's smugness in his voice. "Not to you."

———

"Wake up, Meg." Nightingale's voice.

———

"Wake up, Meg." Noah's voice.

———

"Child, wake up." Clea's voice.

———

"Wake up." Teari's voice.

———

"Maybe you should offer her a beer." Jack's voice.

———

My eyes flash open. There is a black canopy above me. I'm covered with ruby red satin sheets. This mattress is the most comfortable thing that's ever touched my body. I blink a few times until the hazy vision clears, and then I sit up.

I'm in my room in Lucifer's castle.

Someone is sitting on the couch near the far wall. My heart skips, Sparrow? They turn to face me. It's Skeele, dressed in Hellion gear and reading a newspaper with his ankle crossed on his knee. He watches me warily.

"You're awake," Skeele says as he folds his paper and sets it on the couch next to him.

Remembering the voices that pestered me while I slept, I ask, "Where is everyone?"

"They got bored waiting for you to wake up."

"Why are you here?" I move to the edge of the bed.

"I'm here for your safety."

Never needed a Hellion for protection before. My blade did nicely. And my manservant. "Why?"

His brows rise, he picks the newspaper up off the couch and opens it, apparently bored with the conversation. He adds, "Because you're the ruler of Hell now."

Well then.

My stomach growls.

"I'm hungry."

Skeele snaps the fold of his newspaper. "There's food in the fridge."

"Not that kind of hungry." I could drain an army. I could suck every drop of Sparrow's blood without shame.

"That," Skeele peers over his paper at me, "is going to be a problem."

About the Author

M. R. Pritchard is a two-time Kindle Scout winning author and her short story "Glitch" has been featured in the 2017 winter edition of THE FIRST LINE literary journal. She holds degrees in Biochemistry and Nursing. She is a northern New Yorker transplanted to the Gulf Coast of Florida who enjoys coffee, cloudy days, and reading on the lanai.

Visit her website MRPritchard.com and join her newsletter to receive a monthly update on new releases, freebies, current projects, and daily shenanigans of an author's life.

Follow on Amazon to get alerts on new releases.

If you have enjoyed *The Sparrow Man Series*, please leave a review, tell a friend, or gift it to a friend. These small acts keep authors writing. Thank you.

Special Thanks

Thank you so much for reading *Scarecrow*!

To all the fans of *Sparrow Man* who have waited so patiently for this second book in the series, thanks so much for hanging on! I sincerely hope you're enjoying the series; I just love getting lost in Meg and Sparrow's world. There is much more to come. I can't wait to share more of Sparrow and Meg's time together with you.

Help an author out and consider leaving a review or telling a friend about this series. Reviews help readers like you find great books and help writers like me fund another amazing story. And I hope to write many more stories about Meg and Sparrow.

To my friends and family who have supported me; to my husband and daughter who have to put up with me on a daily basis; and to my great friend and awesome editor, Kristy, thank you all so much!

Other Books by M. R. Pritchard

Science Fiction/post-apocalyptic:

The Phoenix Project

The Reformation

Revelation

Inception

Origins

Resurrection

The Phoenix Project Compendium Edition

The Safest City on Earth

The Man Who Fell to Earth

Heartbeat

Asteroid Riders Series

Moon Lord

Collector of Space Junk and Rebellious Dreams

Steampunk:

Tick of a Clockwork Heart

Dark Fantasy:

Sparrow Man Series

Thread the Bone

Fantasy/Fairy Tale Love Story/Romance:

Muse

Forgotten Princess Duology

Midsummer Night's Dream: A Game of Thrones

Poetry/Short Stories

Consequence of Gravity

Raven King
by M. R. Pritchard

Dumb Ways to Die

Meg

Have you ever tried to fly? Takeoff is a bitch. Sparrow made it look easy—heck seagulls make it look easy. Nothing prepares you for the lack of strength in your back, the choking feeling in your throat, the uselessness of your legs, the feeling of purely sucking at life.

"Go!" Skeele shouts. "Launch yourself. Jump! Like this." He catapults himself into the air, his wings whip out and then he's heading toward the Hellsky. Effortless. Like a damned eagle on the coast. Of course, he's big and muscular. I flex my bicep and the smallest muscle bulges. Maybe I should do some push-ups? Skeele lands nearby, the dust of Hell swirls around his boots as he stomps down. "Now," he motions with the swoop of his arm. "It's your turn."

"I'm tired." I cross my arms and tip my head, trying to loosen tense neck muscles.

"You've been sleeping all day." He steps closer. "You shouldn't be tired. You sleep more than a baby." He keeps stepping closer.

Skeele is one big son-of-a-bitch and there was one point in time that he terrified the fuck out of me, but not anymore. Nothing scares the ruler of Hell. I went through too much to fear anyone anymore, even this giant Hellion with horns and sharp teeth.

"Do it, Meg." He's too close. "Fly!" he roars. I jump and take two steps away. "What are you afraid of?" he asks.

I hold out my arms, directing him to stay away. "I just need some space." I roll my shoulders.

"Don't be afraid of failing. None of us came out of the womb with wings. We all had to learn." He's so calm and encouraging, not like the Hellions of the past. He's not like the ones who would rather kill first and ask questions later. Sparrow taught him better.

"I've already failed enough." I roll my shoulders, loosening my back muscles. There's nothing there. It doesn't even feel like anything is thinking of being there. No wings. Nothing.

"Why?" Skeele scoffs. "Because you lost Sparrow?"

"Shut up." I glare at him.

He moves closer. "You're just hangry." Skeele frowns. "I could help you."

I have eaten nearly every Twinkie in Hell, every bag of chips, every orange soda, everything that might send a middle-aged man on a quick trip to cardiac arrest. Nothing will fill my stomach like a little bit of blood would. Like a little sip of Sparrow's blood. But Skeele's blood. No thanks. Not on my life would I drink from him. That's crossing the line.

Skeele's holding out his forearm. The blood pulsing through his thick veins. I can hear it, whoosh-whoosh-whoosh, thundering in my ears. My mouth fills with saliva anticipating the sweet flush of fresh blood. My eyes flick to his face. He's not Sparrow. Not even close. There's no green eyes, no mussed brown hair, no tick of insanity.

"Fucker," I mutter as I stomp away.

"It's not going to go away," Skeele shouts in my direction. "The hunger will never go away. If you don't do something about it, you're going to do something you regret."

Overgrown grass sweeps my legs as I walk to the nearby Jeep Wrangler. I didn't want to practice near the castle, didn't want the others to see that a loser who couldn't fly ruled them. They quivered in the presence of my grandfather. They must do the same for me.

A Northern Flicker whistles a trill from the hood of the Jeep. I stop. These birds keep haunting me. With Sparrow and the others around it was kinda endearing, now every flutter is a sign, every chirp a warning.

"They'll never grow out your back if you don't try," Skeele shouts from the field behind me. "They need an urge to sprout!"

I pick up a rock and throw it at the hood of the Jeep, scaring away the songbird. I gotta get out of here.

The thud of heavy footsteps is suddenly behind me. Large hands grip the waistband of my leather pants and under my arm.

"What the—" I kick, trying to escape but my feet are lifted off the ground.

The fucker doesn't know when to stop. "They'll never appear unless you try," he grumbles in my ear as he tosses me in the air.

My stomach remains on land as I pedal my arms and legs as my eyes scan the treetops.

"No!" I shout as gravity pulls me down.

Skeele is in the air; he grabs the back of my pants again and tosses me higher. "Fly!" he shouts.

My stomach flops like that day Noah and me skipped our exams, stole a car and spent the day at Seabreeze. We rode the Jack Rabbit so many times I puked. I'm ready to puke again. Each time I fall, Skeele tosses me higher and it gets harder and harder to breathe. The air is thin this high up in Hellsky.

He lets me fall over and over again.

"You piece of shit!" I swallow back bile. "I will throw you in the pit for this," I shout.

It's hard to stop your arms and legs from churning in the air. It's not like I have time to reach maximum velocity like in that movie. I twist, my back facing the ground and flip him off.

He's coming at me from above, just far enough away to induce panic. He laughs after glancing at my hands. I wonder for a split second if this is how my grandfather felt as his body fell to the ground. He was gone though. I'd sucked every drop of life out of him.

Skeele grabs me just before I hit the ground.

Fired up, I grab my blade, kick him in the knee and he drops down to kneeling. I slam my foot into the center of his chest and kick him back. Standing on his chest, I set the tip of my blade under his chin.

Read the rest of Raven King on Kindle

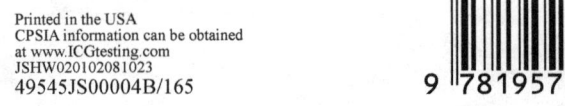